Cupidity

How Not to Spend Your Senior Year
BY CAMERON DOKEY

Royally Jacked
BY NIKI BURNHAM

Ripped at the Seams
BY NANCY KRULIK

Spin Control
BY NIKI BURNHAM

AND COMING SOON:

South Beach Sizzle
BY SUZANNE WEYN AND DIANA GONZALEZ

Cupidity

CAROLINE GOODE

Simon Pulse
New York London Toronto Sydney

SIMON PULSE
An imprint of Simon & Schuster
Children's Publishing Division
1230 Avenue of the Americas
New York, NY 10020

Text copyright © 2005 by John Vornholt

Designed by Ann Zeak
The text of this book was set in Garamond 3.
Manufactured in the United States of America

First Simon Pulse edition January 2005
10 9 8 7 6 5 4 3 2 1
Library of Congress Control Number 2004104828
ISBN-13: 978-1-4169-1147-0
ISBN-10: 1-4169-1147-2

For Richard

Cupidity

One

Flies buzzed around the Dumpster in the alley, and the late-summer heat was brutal even in the shade. Laura Sweeney swatted a mosquito away from her arm and pushed her glasses back up her cute but sweaty nose. Her friend Taryn sat across from her on the benches behind the Dairy Queen, and both were dressed in the blue polyester uniforms of the DQ.

In time-honored lunch break tradition, they weren't eating food from their own establishment; Taryn had just returned with goodies from the 7-Eleven across the street. She gave Laura her chocolate milk and beef jerky, while she opened up a big straw that was full of pink sugar. *Mmmm, lunch.*

"How much do I owe you?" Laura pulled a garish red and yellow wallet from her pocket and handed Taryn a few bucks. The plastic corners were tattered from wear, but the heroic figure of a woman warrior still graced the shiny cover.

Taryn laughed out loud and nearly spit up her sipping sugar. "When are you getting rid of your Xena wallet?" she asked in amazement.

"As soon as I give up the Hercules lunch box," answered Laura proudly. "And speaking of my mythology obsession—I read the most beautiful love story last night. It was about a wood nymph named Egeria, who fell in love with a mortal king named Numa Pompilius." Laura got a wistful look in her eyes, and she took off her glasses. The weeds in the alley didn't look so bad blurry.

"When the king died," she went on, "Egeria was so sad that she couldn't stop crying. Nobody could comfort her, and she wouldn't leave the spot in the woods where they always met. The goddess Diana took

2

pity on Egeria and turned her into water. Her legs became an eternal spring, and her torso shot up into the sky!"

"Wait a minute, hold on," said Taryn, tossing her thick black hair. "The dude dies, and the girl cries so hard that she gets turned into a *fountain*?"

With a sniff, Laura nodded. "That's right."

"And you call that a great love story?" scoffed Taryn. "I'm sorry, but when my boyfriend dies, I don't want to be turned into a fountain. I want to find another guy with a nicer car."

"Well, Egeria wasn't a *girl*," replied Laura defensively. "She was a wood nymph. They used to meet every night in a sacred grove, and she gave him good advice on how to govern his people. They *really* loved each other. I've got the book in my car, if you want to see—"

Taryn reached out, grabbed Laura's arm, and forced Laura back onto the bench. "Girl, you need to get out of these fairy tales and into a reality show. In a week, you're going to be a senior in high school, and have you ever been kissed?"

"Well, of course," said Laura, bristling. "There was that party when we played spin-the-bottle."

"In fifth grade!" snapped Taryn. "Laura, you're pretty—in a bookish kind of way—and there have to be guys who would crawl after you. What about Peter?"

"Peter Yarmench?" asked Laura with a laugh. "Oh, I've known him since we were in kindergarten. He's not my type."

"What *is* your type?" asked Taryn suspiciously.

Laura hugged her beef jerky and smiled dreamily. "Jake Mattson."

Her friend snorted a laugh. "Right, the most popular boy in school. He's *everyone's* type. Can't you aim a little lower than that?"

With a pout, Laura thought about all the boys who really appealed to her, and she came up with another name. "Cody Kenyon. I like *him*."

"The baddest boy in school," muttered Taryn. "I have a hard time seeing you with a bad-boy skater dude."

Laura squared her shoulders and smiled mischievously at her friend. "Is that right?

Well, I'm going to surprise you this year. I'm for sure going to have a boyfriend, and it's going to be whoever I want!"

"Those guys won't even talk to us," said Taryn bitterly. "You need a cheerleader outfit in a size four."

Laura's shoulders slumped and she sat back on the cold cement bench. "Not my style, huh?"

"You're top pick for valedictorian," said Taryn, waving her sugar straw around. "Stick to your own crew—you know, the other valedictorian types."

Laura frowned and put her glasses back on. "Does it always have to be like this? We can never look outside of our usual circle? What if I want something . . . else?"

"Girl, you've got to try *one* boy before you can try them all," said Taryn with a sniff.

Suddenly the back door of the Dairy Queen opened, and a greasy-haired teen stuck his head out. Allen was also wearing a blue polyester uniform, but he had a name badge, which neither one of them had.

"Hey, princesses," he snarled, "your lunch

break was over five minutes ago. I need you to get back to work."

Taryn shot a nasty glance at Allen. "We're expanding our minds by talking about Roman mythology. Do you know anything about that?"

"Heck no," he snapped. "I just know this afternoon is going to be hotter than Hades! We need to inventory before the rush, so hurry up." He ducked back inside, banging the door shut behind him.

Laura chuckled. "'Hotter than Hades.' He knows about mythology, and he doesn't even know he knows. These aren't just fairy tales, Taryn—people worshipped these gods for thousands of years."

"Well, now they worship the mean green," said her friend, rising to her full five-foot-one stature. "That's why we have to work. Come on, back to the custard pits."

With determination, Laura grabbed her chocolate milk and stood up. *This year is going to be different,* she told herself. *I'm going to make sure it is.*

A week later, it was still hotter than Hades, but the school year began as scheduled.

As the first warning bell rang, students streamed into the main door and through the halls of Fimbrey High School in Denton, Ohio, looking for new lockers and old friends. Laura Sweeney had picked out a strategic spot next to the central stairwell, where she could catch sight of everyone going up and down and passing through.

Fimbrey High School didn't require uniforms, but everyone was dressed in a uniform anyway. She picked them out as they walked past: the jocks and preppies in their stylish clothes; the goths and skaters in black shirts, chains, and carefully torn jeans; the homeboys with their super low-rider baggy pants, and the nerdy types, who were the only ones actually obeying the school's dress code.

Laura was a senior this year, which meant that she should be one of the goddesses of the school, but she didn't feel like a goddess. Maybe the sophomores looked up to her, but nobody her own age did, unless they envied future valedictorians. She was carefully showing a little midriff, because she was skinny enough to pull it off. But she didn't show enough skin to get in trouble.

Suddenly the crowd parted, and she could see all heads turning toward a tall, striking blond boy wearing a letter jacket, even though it was way too hot for a jacket. It didn't matter, because Jake Mattson didn't sweat unless he wanted to. Laura moved her glasses farther down her nose—she didn't want to steam them up. She read about Greek gods all the time, but here was one in person. Finally a senior, Jake Mattson really *was* king of the school. Even his girl-friend, Megan Rawlins, looked up to him, although the head cheerleader looked down at everyone else.

Megan got to walk beside Jake, acknowl-edging the greetings from their chosen subjects and ignoring the stares of the peons. The heavenly couple got a snarl from Emma Langdon, a goth chick who wore more eye shadow, piercings, and studs than ten other girls combined. Her cadre of goth-activists snarled along with her, but Jake Mattson ignored the purple-hair crowd. Not everyone was going to like the king, but that didn't change the fact that he still *was* the king.

The skater punks had their own hero,

and he made an entrance, too. Looking like the underworld god Pluto with his shaggy raven hair, skintight T-shirt, and studded jeans, Cody Kenyon strolled down the hallway. Now it was Emma's turn to stare dreamily as the dark lord walked past, carrying his scarred skateboard over his shoulder like a weapon. Curvy little Chelsea Williams hurried after him; clearly, Cody was cool enough to be acceptable even to her popular crowd. Cody gave Chelsea a sneering smile and wrapped his arms around her waist.

Laura wanted to step forward and say something to Jake or Cody, but her feet seemed to be rooted to the spot. Still her mouth was working, and she had once helped Jake with his trigonometry. So she worked up her courage and had lifted her hand to wave hello when a voice boomed behind her.

"Hey, Laura!"

That broke the spell, and she whirled around to see Peter Yarmench, a skinny guy with wavy red hair and numerous freckles. He beamed at her as the royal couple glided past, taking her moment of bravery with them.

"Oh, hi, Peter," she answered, trying to muster some cheer. "How are you?"

"I'm great!" he answered, sounding impossibly cheerful. "I thought school would never start."

And that's why you're so not one of the cool kids, thought Laura. "Yeah, well, here we are again."

"Hey, I called you a bunch of times last week, but you never returned my calls." Peter looked like her puppy when he got caught going through the garbage. She realized it wasn't his fault she was grumpy about school starting this year . . . with *no* romance.

Laura looked away. "Well, I was working really hard down at the DQ." That was a lame answer, she thought, but at least it was partially true.

"Hey, let's see your schedule," he said cheerfully. "Do we have any classes together?"

She fished around in her new planner for her schedule, but she already knew the answer. They would have at least half of their classes together, even though Fimbrey was a big high school with almost two thousand students. For some reason, she and Peter had been joined at the hip ever since first grade, and the scheduling gods never kept them far apart. Of course, they usually took the same advanced classes, and they were competing to be valedictorian.

He grinned as he studied her schedule. "Wow! We've got second period, third period, fifth period, and seventh period. That's amazing!"

"Isn't it?" she replied, mustering a smile. "Who would have thought?"

"I'm looking forward to this year," said Peter with a crooked smile. She peered up at him, thinking he had gotten taller over the summer. "Did they give you a new locker?" he asked.

"Yes, in the old wing by the music room," she answered. "That's good, maybe I won't get trampled."

"Hey, mine's there too!"

The last warning bell rang, and even the slouching homeboys began to hurry a bit toward their first class. Peter looked worriedly at his watch and began to shuffle off. "See you in advanced calculus. Hey, Laura, it's going to be a great year."

She nodded. "I hope so."

Perhaps it was going to be a great year, but it started out like every other year of high school. Laura Sweeney attended all her classes on time and met her new teachers—all of whom were overjoyed to have such a well-regarded student in class. She saw Peter several more times that day, and she ate lunch with Taryn and all her friends from her regular group. She never did work up the courage to talk to Jake Mattson or Cody Kenyon or any of the other boys she didn't already know.

At home, her mom asked her, "How was your day?" and she gave the usual polite but vague answers. She wasn't going to share the fact that the only boy she had had the courage to talk to was Peter Yarmench. Her dad gave her the standard lecture about how this year she had to work harder than ever to keep up her grades, although she knew that her future place at Ohio State was secure. It was only a matter of whether she would be the valedictorian and get some extra scholarship money. Her future looked safe, humdrum, steady as she goes: no excitement, no worries, no big question marks.

And Laura was no closer to getting a boyfriend.

Being the first day of school, there was hardly any homework, so Laura went to her bedroom after dinner to read one of her mythology books. It started to rain, and the warm drops beat a steady rhythm against her window as she read. Although Laura knew the story well, she thrilled at the tale of Pygmalion and Galatea.

Pygmalion was a famous sculptor who created a statue of a woman that was so beautiful that he could love no real woman. When he asked Aphrodite, whom the Romans called Venus, to find him a living mate as beautiful as his creation, the goddess could find none. Taking pity on the lonely sculptor, Aphrodite breathed life into his fantastic statue, and it turned into flesh and blood. Pygmalion named his beloved Galatea, and they married and were deliriously happy for the rest of their lives.

Why can't I have that? thought Laura bitterly. *Why isn't there a perfect boy out there for me? Someone I really like.*

In anguish, she lifted her head and

shouted to the rainy sky, "Jupiter, send me a boyfriend!"

A crack of thunder startled her, and she looked around, feeling a slight chill. Her dog, Chloe, suddenly ran into the room and jumped on the bed, cowering in her arms like she always did when there was loud thunder. Chloe was not a very brave mutt, despite having been named after a brave heroine in mythology.

Laura laughed and scratched her puppy's head. "If only real life were as simple as these fables," she lamented, "but it's so not."

Outside the rain started to fall harder, and the thunder growled a low reply.

TWO

"Mercury! Mister Mercury, wake up!" The desk clerk of the Mount Olympus Retirement Home in Tarzana, California, gently shook the elderly man awake. Mercury was sitting in a wheelchair, his head completely bald except for tufts of white hair around his ears. He was dressed in an undershirt, plaid shorts, and white shoes. A little drool was running from the side of his mouth, and he wiped it on the back of his hand, which was covered with brown age spots. Mercury wasn't just old, he was ancient, and he could be forgiven for moving a little slowly. At four thousand years old, any movement at all was a good thing.

"What?" he rasped. "What is it, Randolph? Time for my nectar?"

"No, no!" exclaimed the desk clerk, a little man with a pencil-thin mustache. He waved a slip of paper in the air. "You got a *message*!"

"A message?" growled Mercury, blinking fully awake. "I haven't gotten a message since . . . what century is this?"

"The twenty-first," answered Randolph.

"My, how time flies." The messenger god blinked fully awake and cast rheumy eyes upon the mortal, who was still a young man, only sixty years old. "You say it was in my *special* box?"

The clerk nodded excitedly. "I didn't open it up—do you want me to?"

"Yes, read it," said the elderly god, sitting up in his chair. They were on the veranda of Mercury's room in the retirement home, and it was a very nice room, if a little old-fashioned. A pair of silver winged slippers hung on the wall, and dusty statues of his family rested on half columns.

The desk clerk tore through the envelope and opened the letter. "It's from a certain Laura Ann Sweeney of Denton, Ohio. It says, 'Jupiter, send me a boyfriend!'"

Mercury bolted upright in his wheelchair. "What? A mortal actually made a plea to Jupiter to find her a boyfriend?"

"That's what it says here," answered Randolph. "Do you want me to throw it away?"

"No, no!" answered the elder. "This is a Heroic Task, and this Laura Sweeney appealed directly to Jupiter, king of the gods! We can't ignore it. Where are the others?"

"Some of them are out by the pool."

"And the big guy?"

Randolph looked over his shoulder. "Jupiter is in the sauna. Do you want me to tell the others?"

"No way. This is *my* job," insisted Mercury. "I'm the messenger god."

"I'll push you out," offered Randolph.

Mercury brushed him off. "No, get me my walker . . . and my winged slippers." As the desk clerk hurried inside to fetch the articles, the elderly god rose uncertainly to his feet. "How long has it been since anyone appealed to the gods?" he mused. "Don't they know we're retired?"

"Semi-retired," corrected Randolph when he returned with the winged slippers and the chrome two-wheeled walker. "You still have a lot of Heroic Deeds left in you!"

"Yes," said Mercury, lifting his chin, which was covered in the stubble of a snow-white beard. "We used to find True Love for mortals all the time. In fact, often we put on disguises and supplied all the love they needed by ourselves." He chuckled with some fond ancient memories.

Randolph placed the walker and the slippers in front of the aged god and stood back. Mercury gripped the arms of the walker to steady himself as he slipped his wrinkled feet into the magical winged footwear. "There, that's better."

A moment later, the desk clerk stumbled backward in awe and alarm, because the centuries began to melt away, revealing an elderly but handsome god. After a while, he didn't look a day over two thousand, though he still had most of his aches and pains.

Gripping the message from Laura Sweeney in his hand, Mercury used his walker to shuffle out to the pool area. On the West Coast, the sun was just beginning to go down, and a soft golden glow suffused the blue pool and the marble pillars that surrounded the water. A warm breeze brought the smell of nectar mixed with Metamucil.

As Mercury approached the swimming pool, he heard the whining voice of Juno, Jupiter's wife. "I told Venus, 'I can't possibly have another lift and tuck,'" she complained, "'or my armpits will be under my ears.'"

Diana nodded, although the elderly goddess of the hunt seemed to be half-listening as she painted her toenails with a long peacock feather. Half a dozen of the graceful birds wandered the grounds, and they outnumbered the gods in attendance. Fat Apollo grumbled under his breath when his foe, Vulcan, made a good shot on the shuffleboard court. In the pool, Neptune splashed around, trying to climb aboard an inflatable raft, but slipping off each time.

None of them noticed the messenger until he had shuffled up right in front of them. "Mercury!" exclaimed Vulcan with surprise. The misshapen god of the forge limped toward him and glanced at his winged feet. "What are you all dressed up for?"

"This!" he crowed, waving the slip of paper in the air. "A mortal has beseeched Jupiter for help. It is a matter of True Love . . . a Heroic Task."

Apollo wheezed. "Are you sure we didn't get that message by mistake?"

"How many Jupiters are there?" asked Mercury.

"Just one," came a raspy voice, and they all turned to see their frail leader, wearing a white terry-cloth robe that seemed to blend in with his long white beard. "Or two, if you count the planet Jupiter. Did we get any royalties from all those planets they named after us? Not a drachma."

Mercury bowed to the elder with the long white beard. "Sire, a mortal has pleaded for your help. Just like the old days—a quest for True Love!" Breathlessly, he told their leader everything he knew about Laura Sweeney and her search for the perfect romance.

"We must handle this correctly," said Jupiter excitedly. His flip-flops smacked the soles of his feet as he paced beside the pool, and he tugged thoughtfully on his flowing beard. "We can't take any chances—we must assign this delicate task to the right hero."

"You mean Venus?" asked Diana, who was always a bit ditzy.

"No! No! Spare us!" cried all the gods at once, jumping to their feet with alarm. "Not Venus!"

Everyone glanced at Vulcan, the brilliant but ungainly god of invention. After all, Venus had wronged him the most. "My ex-wife? You'd be crazy!" he answered. "The less she knows about this, the better."

"Don't worry," said Jupiter, with a wave of his bony hand. "I do not intend to involve Venus, even though this would be easy work for her. Out of spite, she would thwart this mortal because she asked *me* first."

"Her son," suggested Mercury. "Cupid could perform this deed for you."

That brought another scowl to the king's cracked lips. "Yes, matters of love are in his domain, but that cherub is a mercenary and will exact a stiff price."

"Get a grip, husband," said Juno. "If not Venus or Cupid, who will help this maiden? You? Mars? Who?"

Jupiter looked around at the elderly gods gathered beside the sparkling pool and shook his head. "Where is Cupid?"

Apollo pointed over his shoulder and sneered. "At this hour, he likes to hang with mortals at Pinkie's Pool Parlor."

"I might have known." Jupiter heaved a sigh and cast his eyes at Mercury, who was still holding the request from Laura Sweeney in his hand. "Mercury, shall we go fetch him?"

"I have my winged shoes on, don't I?" answered the messenger god with a sniff.

Jupiter snapped his fingers. "Apollo, summon your chariot. But the black limo, not the Hummer."

Twenty minutes later Jupiter and Mercury hobbled into a pit so dank and obscure that Mercury had to light his magic torch just to look around. A rat scurried off along the brown and yellow baseboards, chirping angrily at them, and a putrid draft brought the foul odor of cheap cigar smoke and the aged dust of pool chalk. A maze of dark, rectangular tables confronted the gods, and from somewhere in the bowels of Pinkie's Pool Parlor came a burst of raucous laughter.

Jupiter sneezed, rattling his crown around atop his snowy white mane of hair. He wiped his nose with his long beard and growled, "That mold is playing Hades with my allergies. I say, Mercury, remind me why we're doing this?"

"Laura Sweeney wants a boyfriend, and she appealed directly to you." The frail god clicked his winged slippers and stuck out his chin importantly. "I told everyone about it, and they think we need this heroic task to give our existence a little purpose."

Jupiter groaned and rubbed his rheumy eyes. "Yes, but to bring Cupid out of retirement? I don't know. The world doesn't need him anymore—they have chat rooms!"

Mercury shuffled forward and prodded his old associate in the ribs with a bony elbow. Chuckling, he suggested, "Maybe the mortals need a little more of that old bolt of lightning. You know, that insane, short-circuit jolt that Cupid's arrow used to bring them. We could watch it all in the reflecting pool."

Jupiter nodded and squared his scrawny shoulders. "Lightning bolts," he repeated, as if reminding himself of the mission. With determination, the two elders moved into the dark pathways between the felt-covered slabs of slate. After negotiating the maze, they reached a small circle of light in the far corner, where four men were huddled around a pool table.

Holding court and waving a cigar in the air was Cupid, and his gravelly voice cut through the clack of balls and drone of conversation. The aged cherub, wearing a pith helmet, multipocketed field vest, and stylish hunting clothes, looked ready to go on safari.

His three scurvy companions spotted the aged visitors first, and one brute looked up and laughed. "Who are you guys? Man, the homeless soup kitchen is four doors down."

"We're not lost," said Mercury indignantly. "We're here to talk to your friend." He and the king of the gods turned their attention to the short, squat player with the big cigar.

"I told you guys to leave me alone," said Cupid, while he studied his shot and avoided looking at them. "I'll join the association of retired people when I'm ready, and not before!"

That joke brought a chuckle from the other players, but they scowled when neither Jupiter nor Mercury found it amusing. "Yeah, make an appointment," growled one of the men. "He's busy right now."

As if to prove it, four-foot-tall Cupid stood on his tiptoes, bent over the rail of the pool table, and made a respectable shot, sinking the four-ball in the side pocket.

"You can only stay here if you rent a table," said the smallest of the three mortals, a weasel in a striped suit. "And that costs twenty bucks . . . each." His friends tried to keep a straight face, but two of them laughed.

Jupiter scowled and scratched his long beard. "We really need to talk to Cue here. That is what you call him . . . Cue?"

The diminutive god sank another ball and laughed. "What else would they call me? I'm a pool player. We've got no business together, Old Man. That partnership closed shop . . . long ago."

"One of our old customers," said Jupiter in a hoarse whisper, "has just asked for our help."

That revelation caused Cupid to miscue and awkwardly strike the white ball, sending it on a pathetic spin that avoided every other ball on the table. "Hey!" growled one of the mortals. "You spoiled Cue's shot, and I've got five hundred bucks riding on him! You guys need to get out of here, and I mean *right now.*"

The big human hiked up his jeans and moved threateningly toward the frail elders. "Manny, wait a second," called Cupid, trying to warn his associate.

Jupiter lifted his hand and made a fist, and the entire building began to shake as if besieged by an earthquake. As dust and pieces of plaster rained down on the players, Manny backed up, and his two friends shouted and ran for the exit. Jupiter lowered his hand, having made his point, and the building stopped shaking.

"Whoa!" exclaimed Manny, his mouth agape. "That must've been a five or six on the Richter Scale!" He looked at Cupid and waved his arm. "Let's get out of here, Cue!"

"You go," answered the cherub, chomping on his cigar. "I'll protect these two old codgers."

"Don't wait too long," urged Mercury with a pained grimace. "My bones are aching . . . I feel another one coming on."

The man ducked, looked around furtively, then dashed for the exit. When the door opened, a ray of sunshine invaded the darkness of the pool hall for a moment, then the gloom rushed back. Marooned in a pool of golden light, the three ancient gods stood, waiting.

Shorter than the others and technically a cherub, Cupid still looked young enough to be taken for a mortal. He waved his cigar around the gloom, dispensing smoke like smelly incense. "Okay, you guys have my attention. Who asked for what?"

Excitedly Mercury explained about Laura Sweeney beseeching Jupiter to find her a boyfriend. "A true heroic task!" exclaimed the messenger god, who enjoyed explaining matters. "And we figured you would be the perfect one to help this teenager in Denton, Ohio."

The cherub chuckled. "Did you try my mom yet?"

Jupiter turned as pale as his beard at that question. "Uh, no. She's still upset about that thing between you and Psyche."

"Ah, Psyche," mused Cupid with a wistful smile. "The only woman I ever really loved. You and my mom should not meddle in other people's love lives. That's my job!"

"That's why you're the perfect one for this heroic quest," insisted Mercury, trying to steer the conversation back on track. "Please tell us you'll do it . . . for our reputation."

Cupid shook his head and chomped on his cigar. "I'm not sure about coming out of retirement, Big Guy. Look at me—I haven't strung a bow in years, I'm a little out of shape, and I don't know squat about modern teenagers. For the last two hundred years, I've only seen the insides of pool halls and casinos. I'd have to get into Laura Sweeney's life and get to know her in order to pick the right love for her. That's a lot of work."

"All right," muttered Jupiter with a scowl. "I know something you want. I'll give you back the power to be invisible, even though you misused it."

The fat cherub whirled around, sputtering. "You never should have taken it away from me! When I'm invisible, my job is a slam dunk, but nooooo! You had to run me out of business, you meddling old geezer!"

"We all ran out of business at the same time," insisted Jupiter as he leaned over the pool table, looking all of his four thousand years despite the terry-cloth robe he wore elegantly. "Laura Sweeney is a true fan of ours, or we wouldn't know of her plight. Help her, Cupid, not me. In return, I will give you the cloak you once wore."

"Which my father made for me," muttered Cupid. The cherub blew cigar smoke from the side of his mouth and watched it curl upward into the ancient stains on the ceiling. "How is dear old dad?"

Mercury cleared his throat to show his discomfort with the subject, because no one really knew who Cupid's father was.

Plodding Vulcan was as likely a candidate as most of the other gods and half the mortal world, but the Olympians had a hard time imagining wayward Cupid as his son. Nevertheless, Vulcan had been Venus's husband at the time, and so they behaved as father and son.

The messenger god could see that Jupiter was tongue-tied at the question, and he answered impatiently, "Your sire is excited by this deed, as we all are. He says he can help you with a disguise."

"A disguise?" echoed Cupid, breaking into a mischievous laugh. "Yes, Vulcan can work wonders with his special clay. To get *me* into high school, this will have to be a very special disguise."

Mercury felt a sudden chill on his spine. He had always considered Cupid to be one of the more unstable demigods, and it didn't surprise him that he was still a favorite of the mortals. *He has to be half-mortal*, thought Mercury with a sniff of disdain. *This bargain is going to be trouble, but the pact has been made.*

The king of the gods and the grizzled cherub, who had once been young and lovely when known by the name Eros, gripped each other by the forearm. Overhead the clear California skies growled with an unexpected burst of thunder.

Several days later, Mercury and Jupiter were sent e-mail messages to meet Vulcan by the swimming pool at midnight. Since this was past the bedtime of most of the elderly gods at Mount Olympus, the two cronies had the shimmering water hole to themselves. Or so they thought. When Mercury caught sight of a slender figure breaking the surface of the illuminated water, he grabbed Jupiter's frail forearm.

"Who's that swimming in our pool?" asked Mercury with indignation. "Another rotten neighborhood kid, I suppose." Jupiter shrugged, and both of them squinted into the darkness.

When the mysterious swimmer emerged from the water and climbed up the ladder, Mercury gasped. Even in the suffused light from the pool, he could see it was a maiden of unearthly beauty. After tossing back her glistening blond hair, she wrapped a silky robe around her body and strode toward them. Jupiter gripped the messenger god's forearm, trying to steady himself.

The girl was young, and her beauty was brought down to earth by a wide-eyed innocence and appealing trust. "Hello, my lords," she said with a lilting voice and a graceful curtsey. "My master will arrive any second, and he is eager to see you."

"And Cupid arrived at Vulcan's laboratory, as planned?" asked Jupiter.

"I believe so, because Vulcan has been occupied," answered the fair maiden.

He must be sorely occupied to leave you alone, thought Mercury. The messenger god wanted to say something witty to this marvelous creature, but he was as tongue-tied as a mortal. A shuffling of footsteps could be heard on the walkway, and he turned to see the slow arrival of the god of invention, Vulcan.

"Hello, Brother!" called Jupiter as the hunched, deformed immortal hobbled toward them. "We were just being entertained by, uh . . . by your lovely assistant. What is her name?"

"I haven't named her yet," replied Vulcan,

making it sound as if such details were a bother. Mercury cringed, because there were often disastrous results when Vulcan fabricated a female. He shivered at the memory of Pandora, who had let her wicked curiosity ruin the world. This time, he hoped, Vulcan's art would have less drastic effects.

Jupiter finally said, "I had hoped to find Cupid here."

"That is no problem," said Vulcan with a wink at his fair assistant.

The girl chuckled, her voice sounding like wind chimes; then she punched the frail god in the ribs and nearly doubled him over. "I *am* Cupid, you old sot."

Jupiter groaned and peered at her in amazement. Mercury felt his stomach knot and shrivel, because no good could come of this ruse. "Nice disguise, huh?" asked Cupid, turning about and giving them a good look at the rest of "her" godly figure.

Mercury gulped. "I think, uh . . . you had better be very careful in that disguise."

"I'm the god of love," sniffed Cupid. "I know my business."

Vulcan wagged a crooked finger at her.

"Remember what I told you—this maiden disguise is only good for twenty-five days. On midnight of the twenty-fifth day, the clay will dissolve, leaving you with your regular appearance."

"You worry too much," said Cupid with a charming shake of her hips. "Twenty-five days will be plenty of time to handle this job. Now where's my bow? You refurbished it, right?"

"Yes, yes," answered Vulcan wearily. "New string, fewer jewels, and pearl inlay. I still couldn't make it look like a modern bow, but it no longer looks like a one-string harp. And your arrows have all been reflected."

"Good." The blond enchantress moved close to Jupiter and batted her lashes at him as her dazzling blue eyes drilled into his. "Jupiter, from you I need a nice purse full of credit cards, car keys, and other useful goodies. I'll need a few days to set this up—I'll start school next Monday." She frowned, and a cloud crossed her precious face. "Uh-oh, do I have to deal with . . . feminine products?"

As if appeasing a bratty child, Vulcan

sighed. "No, Cupid. We figured you couldn't handle such matters with any maturity. Hence, twenty-five days."

"Oh good. Fine. That's plenty of time anyway," said the lovely cherub with a confident smile. "Laura Sweeney, you are about to get some serious love in your life."

Three

"Have you seen her?" came frantic whispers in the hallway of Fimbrey High School. Boys were gathering in tight-knit groups all over the place. "You've got to see her. She's off the hook!"

"Who? Who are you talking about?" came the eager replies.

"The new girl!" hissed one of the guys. "She's got it goin' on."

"And she just moved here," added another one. "No ties, no baggage . . . She doesn't know a soul!"

Laura and Taryn waded through the crowded hallway, and every guy they passed seemed to be extolling the charms of the new girl. Laura had seen this phenomenon before, of course. The New Girl or New Boy was one of the few elements of surprise that could perk up what would otherwise be the ordinary high school day.

"The new girl . . . the new girl . . . ," mimicked Taryn. "There's nine hundred girls in this school, but the boys see us every day, so we're invisible. Then comes some new chick they haven't been staring at since first grade, and they're drooling all over themselves!"

"She'll be exotic for a day," said Laura, "but by tomorrow they'll stick her into one of the normal groups. She'll be the 'old girl' then. We should try to catch a glimpse before she turns into one of us."

Taryn reached out a hand to stop her friend, and her eyes darted behind them. "We may have a chance," she whispered. "Here comes the Welcoming Committee, and they look none too happy about the competition."

Laura turned to see Megan and Chelsea leading a mob of about ten irate popular girls. Down the hallway they marched with fierce determination in their eyes, and

Taryn grabbed Laura's arm and dragged her into the procession.

After a moment, Chelsea looked back at Laura and Taryn, and her eyes blinked with surprise. "What are you trailing along for?" she asked. "You haven't got boyfriends to protect."

"Protect from what?" asked Laura, playing innocent.

Taryn laughed. "Don't tell me Cody is sniffing around this new girl?"

A little too quickly, Chelsea snapped, "Of course not."

Taryn gave Laura a wink, and they both quickened their step to keep up with the swarm of enraged cheerleaders. Led by Megan, the mob swept down the corridor until they spotted their target—a bunch of boys huddled around a tiny figure in front of a locker. Laura recognized Jake Mattson, Cody Kenyon, and half a dozen other popular seniors, but she couldn't get a good look at the object of their attention. All she caught was a shimmer of blond hair.

Laura also unexpectedly glimpsed a familiar face on a gangly body, hovering back a few feet but using his height to check out the attraction. A second later, as if hearing her footsteps in the crowded hallway, Peter Yarmench turned and glanced directly at Laura. But before she could say anything, she was distracted by an audible female growl.

Like a heat-seeking missile, Megan Rawlins zoomed toward Jake and the dazed crowd of boys. Sensing danger, the ones on the outside scattered to let Jake and Cody take the brunt of the attack. Megan's steely glare said it all; she was still the school's reigning queen, and she wasn't giving it up easily.

For the first time, Laura got a good look at the new girl. *Whoa,* she thought, *she's drop-dead, movie-star gorgeous!*

As the other girls had the same revelation, they skidded to a stop. In the presence of this petite but shapely hottie, dressed in the latest couture threads and showing off abs of steel, they were stunned. To her credit, Megan somehow went on with her mission.

"Jake," she said, putting sweet daggers around his name, "you were supposed to meet me outside biology."

"Uh, yeah . . . right . . . s-sorry," he stammered, reluctantly tearing his attention away from the fresh face smiling sweetly at him. "But we were just making our new arrival feel comfortable. She doesn't know anybody at Fimbrey."

"Oh, that's too bad," said Megan, doing her best to look unimpressed by the stunning beauty in front of her. "We'll make sure that she learns everything she needs to know to get along here at Fimbrey."

"What's your name?" asked Chelsea, sounding as if she hoped the new girl would at least have an ugly name.

The girl thought for a moment, flipped her perfect hair, and answered, "Cupidity. You know, like Charity or Felicity."

"Or Stupidity," joked Megan, getting an uneasy laugh from her girlfriends.

For the first time, Cupidity looked a bit annoyed, and her dazzling blue eyes narrowed at Megan. "That's not very nice," she remarked.

Megan crossed her arms and shot a cutting glare at the newcomer. "I'll tell you what's not very nice—moving in on somebody else's territory!" She grabbed Jake's arm possessively and held him tightly, even though he shrugged uncomfortably.

"We were only talking!" he protested.

Megan ignored his defense, never taking her steely eyes off the competition. "Cupidity, you've got to decide whether you're with the program or against it. One word of advice: Pick your friends very carefully."

Cupidity looked thoroughly confused by Megan's veiled threats. "Uh, I just want to make friends," she answered with pert innocence. "That's the only program I'm with."

Chelsea sniffed and turned to leave, grabbing Cody Kenyon's arm. "Are you coming, baby?"

As the closest thing the cool crowd had to a bad boy, Cody had more latitude to break the rules. "I'm leaving, but not with you," he told her. Until five minutes ago, Chelsea had been the great love of his skater-boy life, but now he ditched her with a sneer. With all this attention around, he had a large audience—including the new girl—and he squared his black-clad shoulders and sauntered coolly into the crowd.

Chelsea broke into tears, and her friends

gathered around to comfort her. This bad vibe, along with a warning bell, seemed to signal the end of the hallway confrontation. Everyone headed off in different directions, and Taryn waved good-bye too as she hurried off to class. For some reason, Laura hung back to study the petite force that had just invaded the school, even when the bells warned her that she would be late.

She was fascinated by anyone who stood up to Megan, Chelsea, and the other queen bees, and Cupidity had done so without even breaking a sweat. As the newcomer peered into her locker, Laura felt a shadow pass them. She turned to see Megan, who had returned.

"Oh, you two are hanging together," said Megan with a sneer and a laugh. "I might have known. Just what this school needs—another brain!" Megan ambled her way down the hall, waving her hall pass and turning her back to them.

Cupidity reached into her locker and pulled out a small bow and arrow, which she aimed at Megan's back.

"Whoa there!" exclaimed Laura, jumping between Cupidity and her target. She quickly grabbed the bow and stuffed it back inside the locker, whispering, "What's the matter with you? You can't bring *weapons* to school!"

"It's just a little bow," protested Cupidity. "When I use it, there's hardly any blood."

"Do you want to get kicked out your first day of school?" Laura sighed and slammed the locker door shut. "Now promise me you won't go waving any more weapons around."

"It's really a bad idea?" asked Cupidity innocently.

"Yes, a very bad idea," said Laura. "Where did you go to school before this . . . Middle-earth?"

"I was, uh . . . homeschooled," answered the newcomer. "Private tutors all the way."

"Lucky you," said Laura. This girl was definitely odd, but Laura sensed that she was honestly confused and overwhelmed, despite all the attention from the guys. So she held out her hand. "I'm Laura Sweeney."

At that simple declaration, the girl's blue eyes widened like hubcaps on a

Hummer. "Laura Sweeney! I was hoping to meet you!" She eagerly shook her outstretched hand.

Laura smiled, but asked suspiciously, "Me? Why did you want to meet *me*?"

"Uh, because," stammered Cupidity with a frown, "I heard you, uh, could help me with my grades."

"It's your first day. How bad can your grades be?"

"I had lots of tutors, remember." Cupidity smiled hopefully. "I have a good feeling about you, Laura. So many people want to be my friend, because . . . well, I'm gorgeous. But you seem down to earth, like there's more to you than the usual boy-crazy teenagers. Of course, I often have lots of boys hanging around."

Laura shrugged. "Yeah, and you certainly haven't made many friends among the other girls here. You weren't really going to shoot Megan Rawlins with a bow and arrow, were you?"

Cupidity gave a lilting laugh. "Oh, no, that's just my way of taking out frustration. My therapist told me to do symbolic acts like that. I wasn't going to hurt her, honest." She looked around the empty hall-way. "So are we late to class?"

"Very," answered Laura glumly. "At least you have an excuse, being new. We'd better stop by the office and get a hall pass."

"Oh, thank you," said Cupidity, grant-ing her insta-friend a sparkling grin. "We're going to be super close, I can tell!"

Laura shook her head, wondering if this would be a blessing or a curse.

After school, the boys were still falling down steps to get a good look at Cupidity. She was totally surrounded. Even Cody and Jake had ditched their former loves to fol-low the new girl around. To her credit, Cupidity didn't play favorites with them or anyone else; she was unfailingly friendly to everyone she met. Even a few of the girls seemed to be warming to her, but Megan and Chelsea were nowhere to be seen in the crowd on the edge of the parking lot.

Laura watched from a safe distance, although she was supposedly going home with Cupidity after school. That was going to stun everyone when they saw her stroll off with the hot new chick, but Laura had mixed feelings about her fast friendship with the newcomer. For one thing, she was carrying Cupidity's duffel bag, and she could feel the distinct outline of her bow and the sharp tips of her arrows, which could get them both into a lot of trouble.

That's ironic, thought Laura, *a girl named Cupidity being into archery, even if it is only symbolic.* She shrugged and decided, *Probably no one but me would get that.*

Laura felt a familiar presence hovering behind her, and she turned to see Peter Yarmench staring over the top of her head. "Hey, Laura, do you think you could maybe introduce me to your friend?" he asked. "Maybe when there aren't four hundred other guys around."

"You, too?" she remarked with a sigh. "Well, I don't really know how long she and I will be hanging out, but I'll try. You might have to get at the end of the line, and it's a long line."

"Oh, come on, don't count me out," said Peter. "She likes you, so maybe she likes the brainy type. She smiled at me in the lunchroom. Besides, after this summer, I'm not as shy as I used to be."

Laura turned around expecting to find him staring at Cupidity and her admirers, but instead he was gazing at her with a mysterious smile. He quickly glanced away, though, and shifted on his feet, looking as shy as ever. "Anyway," he went on, "if you two want to form a study group or anything, call me."

"I think she could definitely teach us a few things," said Laura. "So tell me, what about this summer?"

Peter smiled enigmatically. "Oh, up at the lake, when my folks and I were at the cottage."

"You met someone?"

"*Two* someones," he answered with a smile. "You know, it's a lot different to meet a girl *outside* of high school, when you don't have all those years of history. You're just *you*. You know what I mean?"

"Yes," Laura answered with a wistful nod. "A fresh start."

"That must be what it's like for Cupidity to start over here," said Peter. Again he peered over Laura's head at the new star of Fimbrey High. "Hey, she's coming this way! She waved to us!"

"I hope so, I've got her stuff." Laura waved back and hefted the duffel bag.

Jake Mattson broke off from the others, proudly waving a slip of paper in the air. "I'll call you later, Cupidity!" he shouted, loudly enough for everyone to hear.

Peter licked his fingers and tried to stick down a cowlick at the crown of his head. "Will you introduce me to her, please?"

"Okay."

Laura tried to introduce her old friend to her new friend, but everyone was talking at once and moving off toward their cars, rushing to escape from school.

Peter said something, and Cupidity grinned and answered, "Cool to meet you, too, Peter. Any friend of Laura's is one of mine, too."

"Hey, Sweeney!" shouted a voice from the crowd; it sounded like Chelsea. "We'll remember the way you turned on us!"

What does that mean? Laura whirled around, trying to find the source of the shout. Maybe she had misunderstood, because it was noisy in the parking lot.

With her heart beating faster, Laura darted ahead of her friend. "Where are we going?" she asked with concern.

"Right here." Cupidity halted at a sleek yellow convertible, which looked brand-new. In fact, it still had dealer's plates on the back, as if it had just come from the showroom. The crowd of stragglers came to a stop and stared as she and Cupidity climbed into the beautiful car. This was not the type of vehicle people in Denton, Ohio, drove, and Laura guessed that it was Italian, maybe a Ferrari or a Lamborghini.

She didn't usually attract attention, so Laura felt funny with half the school watching her as she drove off with her new friend. She hoped Taryn, Peter, and the others understood, but *somebody* had to take this exotic creature under their wing. Cupidity couldn't be left entirely to the mercy of Cody, Jake, and every other boy in school. At least one girl had to befriend her.

No good deed goes unpunished, thought Laura. *It's taken me twelve years, but I've finally made enemies of Megan, Chelsea, and the whole clique.*

Tires squealing, Cupidity roared out of

the parking lot, cutting in front of several other cars and barely missing the gate and the crossing guard. Laura sank into her seat, but the top was down and everybody could still see her, especially the old crossing guard, who was yelling his head off.

"Hey, this is a school zone," he reminded the driver.

"Well, duh!" answered Cupidity, then turned to face Laura. "So the first day of school was fun. How do you think I did?"

"How did you do?" asked Laura with surprise. "You mesmerized half the school and made the other half furious at you. Do you know what effect you have on guys?"

Cupidity smiled. "I've always been lucky at love. My birthday is Valentine's Day."

"Why does that not surprise me?" said Laura, shaking her head. "You know, Jake and Cody and some of those guys had girlfriends . . . before you came."

"I know their kind," scoffed Cupidity. "I've seen them a million times—heroes already posing for their statues. They're too in love with themselves to really be in love with anyone else, but they're the most fun to mess with."

Laura peered curiously at her new friend, thinking that she had a weird way of talking, but that she'd certainly make senior year interesting.

"We're here!" announced Cupidity, pulling the yellow sports car into the driveway of an elegant apartment complex. "I thought it would be best to live close to school."

Laura breathed a sigh of relief, because she had been certain that Cupidity would live in a huge mansion. These were nice apartments, but still apartments. The new girl parked the car, grabbed her duffel bag, and jumped out, while Laura grabbed her backpack and followed meekly. A few seconds later, they walked into a fantastic apartment that looked freshly painted and was furnished with all new stuff. In fact, Laura could still smell the paint, and she saw a price tag on one of the lamps.

"You really did just move here, didn't you?" asked Laura, looking for a place to sit. All of the couches and chairs were elegant leather and appeared as if they hadn't even been sat on yet. She finally picked a big armchair, and dropping into it felt as if she were oozing into a vat of butter.

"How come you moved to Denton?" asked Laura. "Did one of your parents get transferred?"

"My parents aren't here," announced Cupidity as she went to the refrigerator. "I live alone. Do you want a soda?"

It wasn't easy to bolt upright in the cushy leather chair, but Laura managed to sit up. "Did you say you live alone? *By yourself?*"

"Yeah," answered Cupidity as she returned with two sodas. "I don't see the need for parents; they just get in the way."

Through her brave smile, it seemed that a tear welled in the corner of a dazzling blue eye. Laura looked at her friend with concern and asked, "Is something the matter?"

Cupidity nodded and lowered her voice to answer, "Parents have always been a sore subject with me. My mother was a party girl, and I haven't seen my father in a while. They have money, of course, and I've had the best of everything. Now a rich uncle looks after me and rents me this place. You won't tell the school board, will you, that I live alone?"

"No, of course not!" Laura laughed nervously. The idea of a high school student living like an adult was exciting but also somewhat frightening. Then again, Cupidity seemed mature beyond her years, and she looked as if she could take care of herself. Maybe she would shoot any intruders with her bow and arrow.

Laura leaned forward, choosing her words carefully. There was no way to ask this politely, so she just came out with it. "Cupidity, you know you could be friends with *any* of the girls at school, including all the really popular ones. Why would you choose to be friends with *me*?"

"Lacking a little self-esteem, are we?" asked her hostess with a sympathetic smile. "I don't see *you* hanging out with Megan and Chelsea and their herd of water buffaloes. Who can blame you? It's mentally tiring being around that many snobs. Besides, there's only room in the school for one queen, and Megan just got dethroned."

"Totally," answered Laura. "You can be the new ruler of Fimbrey High."

"Me?" scoffed Cupidity. "Not me . . . *you*!"

"*Me?*" squeaked Laura. "You just met me, but haven't you realized yet that I'm not exactly the Homecoming Queen type?"

"But you like that type of guy, don't you?" asked Cupidity with a sly wink. "Which one do you really want? Jake? Cody? That other boy you introduced me to—Peter? You can take your pick."

Laura gulped in embarrassment. "Now you're making fun of me. I don't have a boyfriend, and Jake and Cody are way out of my league."

"That's why you have *me* around, to give you a little help. Why don't we try them out first, and then decide."

The telephone suddenly rang, making Laura jump. Cupidity gave a merry laugh and said, "That should be Jake calling . . . right on cue."

She picked up the cordless phone from the coffee table and said, "Hello?" After a moment, she smirked. "Yeah, I knew it was you, Jake. Of course I want to go out with you . . . tomorrow night."

While Cupidity chatted, Laura was relieved to have a second to think about what she'd been saying. Why was the new girl so intent on hooking her up and making her "queen"? It was kinda sweet, but definitely bizarre.

As if she were reading Laura's mind, Cupidity winked again at her and said into the phone, "But I want to double-date, Jake. I want my friend, Laura Sweeney, to go with us."

Now Laura jumped to her feet and waved her hands, but Cupidity ignored her. "I don't care who it is," she said, "you know all the guys. Pick one Laura would like—a hot date!"

Laura circled the couch and felt like pulling her hair out. True, her new friend was just trying to do her a favor, but being on a double date with Jake Mattson was going to be seriously bizarre. Cupidity laughed softly at something Jake said. Apparently Jake was so smitten that he had agreed to go on a double date with one of the dorks. It was hard to believe.

When Cupidity finally hung up the phone, Laura just stared at her. "Why did you do that?"

"To get to know Jake better," answered Cupidity with a flip of her blond hair.

"Don't you want to get to know Jake better?"

"Yeah, but . . . umm, I have parents, and they might not want me to go out on a Tuesday night." Laura began to pace again. Dating wasn't a common occurrence for her, especially not with Jake Mattson. In truth, her parents wouldn't mind at all if she went on a double date—they would probably open a bottle of champagne!

"Face it, Laura," said Cupidity, "from now on, your life is going to have a little romance in it." She laughed happily, as if enjoying a private joke.

Laura could only shake her head and wonder what she had gotten herself into. Cupidity was a trip, and she definitely had that wonderful new-girl quality of having no preconceptions. *For some reason, she thinks boys should be chasing me,* thought Laura, *and I hate to discourage that idea.*

Four

Cupidity's second day at Fimbrey was a bit more sane, because the novelty had worn off . . . a little. Cupidity picked Laura up in her shiny convertible and took her to school, where Cody Kenyon met them in the parking lot. It had gotten around at the speed of light that Cupidity was going out with Jake Mattson, which had scared off most of the other boys, but not the bad-boy skater dude.

Cody strode right up to the car and asked, "Cupidity, what's this I hear about you going out with Jake Mattson? Dude, that's scraping the bottom of the barrel."

The newcomer laughed. "Oh, is it? Not

all the girls around here think so. Besides, it's only *one* date, and I have lots of nights open."

Cody's eyes sparkled, even while Laura rolled her eyes. He came closer to Cupidity and whispered, "Oh, so we could like . . . meet up another time?"

Cupidity shrugged and gave him an enigmatic smile. She hadn't promised him anything, thought Laura, but he looked as if he had won the lottery. She pointed into the distance, and they all turned to see Jake coming, followed by another guy. Cody nodded and flung his skateboard to the pavement; he jumped on while it was still moving and careened off between the cars.

"Silly, aren't they?" said Cupidity, giving Laura a sly smile. "Are you sure you want one?"

Laura gulped, unsure what her new friend meant by that. *Is it that apparent that I want a boyfriend? Does she think she's doing me a favor?*

"Oh, it's your friend, too!" Cupidity waved to the boys walking toward them, and Laura adjusted her glasses to get a good look. She had to blink twice, because it looked like Peter Yarmench hurrying to keep up with Jake Mattson. They seemed to be walking together.

Laura wrinkled her nose into a puzzled expression and turned to Cupidity. "I don't get it—Peter and Jake?"

The boys were only a few feet away, and Laura marveled that Peter was taller than Jake and only a little skinnier. Her old friend was dressed in his best impression of a preppy, and she almost laughed out loud.

Jake pouted at Cupidity and asked, "Hey, who were you talking to?"

"Anybody I want," she answered cheerfully. "Don't act like you own me, Jake. Come 'ere. I want to talk with you a sec." She motioned coyly for him to follow her, and he did, leaving Laura and Peter alone.

Peter looked only slightly less confused than she did, and he finally said, "You know I'm your date tonight, right?"

Laura tried not to slap her head and say, "D'oh!" Instead she mustered a smile and answered, "I didn't know it would be *you*. Listen, Peter, this wasn't *my* idea. I didn't want to go on a date with Cupidity and Jake."

"Why not?" asked Peter with surprise. "This is great! All of a sudden, you're best friends with the hottest girl in school, and *Jake Mattson* calls me up and wants a favor. We just jumped about three rungs on the social ladder, and I don't know how we did it. But I don't think we should complain about it." He smiled slightly. "Besides, I think you can suffer through one date with me."

"That's not what I meant." Laura caught Peter looking past her at Cupidity and Jake, who were huddled close together near the hood of her car. "You like her too, don't you?"

"Well, uh . . . what's not to like?" stammered Peter. "She's beautiful and funny, and there's something different about her. I know you like Jake—you always have." Peter laughed, and Laura had to laugh along with him at their ridiculous plight.

"Okay," she admitted, "us going out with the beautiful people is kind of funny. I guess we should enjoy it while it lasts."

"Which may not be long," whispered Peter.

"Why not?"

He pointed to a group of girls lurking near the hedges that ran along the parking lot. "Megan Rawlins, Chelsea Williams, and their crew are spying on us," explained Peter. "Well, maybe not *us* . . . more like Jake and Cupidity."

Laura sighed. "And when they get their revenge, it won't be funny, will it?"

"So let's enjoy it while it lasts," suggested Peter with a smile. "And let's agree to always stay friends, no matter what happens."

With relief, Laura nodded, and it was great to feel that she had at least one ally in this crazy adventure. She heard footsteps and she turned to see that Cupidity and Jake had rejoined them.

"We were just deciding what to do on our date tonight," said Cupidity, flipping her blond hair. Laura noticed that she did that a lot—and that it usually caused the boys' jaws to drop. "I hope you don't mind if I picked something."

"No, sure, anything you want!" said Peter quickly.

Jake looked down and cleared his throat. "I wanted to go bowling or maybe to a movie, but Cupidity wanted to do something a little different."

"Like what?" asked Laura hesitantly.

"Archery," answered Jake, looking puzzled.

"It's fun!" insisted Cupidity. "I know a great little place where they rent bows. You'll all be hitting the bull's-eye in no time."

"Archery!" exclaimed Peter, faking enthusiasm, or maybe he really was enthusiastic about doing any activity with Cupidity. "We'll be like the elves in *Lord of the Rings*!"

"Whatever." Jake rolled his eyes, but he looked resigned to following Cupidity's orders along with the rest of them. Then again, she hadn't really done anything the three of them should complain about.

Laura peered curiously at her petite friend. "You're really into bows and arrows, aren't you?"

"You never know when you gotta hunt big game," she answered with a wink.

That night Peter came to Laura's house to officially pick her up for the date, and her parents made themselves scarce. All they requested was a ten-thirty curfew, being a school night, and then the parental units disappeared. Peter hemmed and hawed but smiled a lot and seemed to be enjoying this unexpected fling with the old king and the new queen of the popular crowd.

"And Jake says that maybe I can be the manager of the basketball team," bragged Peter proudly. "He says he can swing it with the coach, him being the star of the team and all."

Laura tried not to roll her eyes, because she was sure that Jake would have promised Peter anything to make this date happen. Now that it was happening, they were both expendable, but she didn't tell him that. Instead she grabbed his arm and convinced herself to have fun on this date, no matter what happened.

Descending the steps, Laura gasped when she caught sight of the dazzling couple in the glow of a streetlamp. Cupidity had let Jake drive the convertible, and he was basking in glory with the sleek sports car and beautiful blond under his apparent command. Cupidity and Jake both had glistening hair that was wind-blown and electrified from the night air, and their cheeks bore a rosy glow. *They look like the costars of a teen chick flick,* thought Laura glumly. *How can I have a chance with Jake?*

Cupidity squealed and waved at her, and Laura was cheered by the fact that her newest friend was still acting like her best friend. But it also made her think of Taryn, which brought a twinge of guilt. Laura plastered a smile onto her face, especially for Jake, and she and Peter climbed into the open back seat of the convertible. With Peter's long legs, it was cramped back there, and their limbs pressed against each other no matter how much they shifted around.

When the car roared off, Laura forgot all the cramped seating in the rush of wind. She had spent half an hour fixing her hair, which was a long time for her, and the wind blew it into a tumbleweed shape in a few seconds. By the time they reached the next stop sign, Laura had severe convertible hair, while Cupidity and Jake still possessed perfect locks.

Peter looked at her and tried not to

laugh. His wavy red hair was now wild, but it was still kind of cute. "Tell me it will be dark at this place," whispered Laura, trying to corral her unruly locks with a hair band. "Wherever we're going."

He shrugged. "Archery—that's all I know. I don't think Jake plans to stay there long. He has other ideas."

"I bet he does." Laura worried that those in the front seat would hear them, but she could barely hear Peter in the fast-moving convertible. Cupidity yelled something over her shoulder, and her words were completely lost in the blast of wind. Still it was fun being outside, under the stars, *on a date*!

Jake said something that made Cupidity laugh, and she pointed off to the right. A moment later, they turned down a rather lonely country road, and Laura and Peter exchanged puzzled glances. If she didn't know how avidly Cupidity wanted to do archery, Laura would have thought they were headed down this deserted road in order to reenact a 1950s make-out movie and go "parking." Peter laughed nervously and tugged at the collar of his shirt, and

Laura was glad to see another car following them.

After driving through a stand of dark trees, they passed a high metal fence that had some weird murals on it—crossed sabers, rifles, and bows. Behind the fence, the lights were so bright that Laura wondered if the place was a junkyard. Seconds later, they slowed in front of a large gate and a sign that read, WAR GAMES COMBAT CAMP.

As they crunched along slowly on the gravel, she heard Jake say, "Yeah, I came here once to play paintball."

"I've heard of it," Laura admitted, but she had always thought it was a front for some illegal militia.

Even though Jake had been here before, he didn't seem anxious to drive in until Cupidity ordered him. "Go on in, you silly," she insisted. "They won't bite."

Peter looked at Laura and gulped, and they both managed a nervous smile. "I don't want to wound anybody on our first date," said Laura.

"Me neither," squeaked Peter. "Cupidity, you'll show us what to do, right?"

"Oh, sure," she answered eagerly. "It's

like really simple—be careful where you shoot, and don't shoot unless you're prepared to accept the consequences."

"What consequences?" asked Jake with a sneer. "I always hit what I'm aiming at."

"Me, too," answered Cupidity with a saucy smile.

When the purring sports car rumbled onto the spacious grounds, Laura saw why they needed so many lights. At least a dozen pretend soldiers in camouflage fatigues were running around a paintball field that looked like a sparse junkyard. Here and there sat old vehicles, large shipping crates, stacks of tires, and other found objects that gave the participants cover as they lumbered around. Laura could hear the metallic thuds of the paintball guns, and she heard the cries of outrage when someone was hit and had to leave the game.

The archery range wasn't nearly as large, and it was kind of crude, with the bull's-eye targets mounted on bales of hay in the distance. There was also a regular shooting gallery, which was dark at this late hour, and a driving range where four golfers were hooking balls into a great stretch of dirt. Whoever owned this acreage was making the most of it, considering that it was nothing but a lot of dirt, a few trees, and some old junk.

Cupidity leaped out of the car and ran to an old wooden building, where two men were lounging on the porch. Like males everywhere, they jumped to attention when she approached, and they seemed to know her. She showed them her ornate bow, and one of them marveled over it, while the other went to fetch some regular bows. Meanwhile, she nocked one of her own arrows, and tested the tautness of the string.

Jake killed the engine in the convertible and turned to the passengers in the back seat. "I know this is a funky place," he whispered. "Don't worry, we're not going to stay here any longer than we have to . . . unless she wants to take a walk in the woods. I'd be up for that. How about you guys?"

"You lead, and we'll follow," answered Peter meekly. Laura just shrugged and tried to look game for anything. In truth, she wanted to see Cupidity shoot her precious bow and arrow more than she wanted to walk in the ominous woods. Looking at this surreal scene, Laura thought that it might not be such a bad thing that she never "dated." Dates were like reality TV shows—some of them were just determined to go wrong.

"Come on, guys!" called Cupidity as she motioned them over to the archery range. One of the workers traipsed along to show them how to nock an arrow and shoot a bow, but it wasn't difficult. The long ones required lots of strength, but the compound bow mostly required concentration, cool nerves, and good aim. Laura found out she was pretty good with it, and she surprised herself by enjoying the archery contest.

At one point, Jake scored last out of the four of them, and Laura saw the ugly competitive side of her Greek god. He challenged them to another round and forced Laura and Peter to use regular long bows, as he did. Laura couldn't muster the strength to be very accurate with the old-fashioned weapon, and she finished dead last. She didn't know for sure, but it appeared as if Peter threw the match to

Jake and let him finish second. As usual, Cupidity whipped all of them with her peculiar harp-shaped bow.

In fact, Cupidity was a deadly shot, and she peppered her targets on the old bale of hay. Her arrows weren't always bull's-eyes, but she was in the general vicinity, unlike the rest of them, who kept sailing arrows into the bushes. After every round, Cupidity carefully collected her spent arrows, and Laura got the impression that they were as rare as her bow.

The girl's skills were so amazing that she collected a small crowd of onlookers, mostly paintballers just getting off the field. A few of them hung back in the shadows, watching from a distance, and Cupidity put on a show for them. Jake tried again to beat her and only made a fool of himself.

As they walked through the muddy parking lot, Jake muttered darkly about going bowling the next time. It was clear that he didn't like to be shown up by anyone, not even the remarkable Cupidity. Laura wasn't sure that there would be a next time with Jake and Cupidity. Despite looking gorgeous together, they didn't seem to have much chemistry, or much in common.

Laura smiled at Peter and gripped his hand, and he gave her a gentle squeeze. *Peter would make a low-maintenance boyfriend,* she decided, *unlike Jake, who would be a royal pain.*

Without warning, two paintballers jumped out of the shadows and fired a barrage of colorful orbs at Cupidity. Bright green and purple gobs exploded all over her clothes like neon spaghetti sauce. A paintball caught Laura in the shoulder and splattered purple paint on her glasses. She yelped, because it stung. Cupidity tried to dodge the attack, but there was no place to run—several messy shots found their mark. Jake dove for cover behind a car, while Peter jumped in front of Laura and stopped two more projectiles intended for her. But they weren't shooting at the boys.

Since the ambushers wore protective masks and army fatigues, it was impossible to make out their faces, but Laura recognized their malicious giggles. When they shot paint all over the beautiful yellow convertible, she knew it had to be Megan and Chelsea. Still shrieking with laughter, the attackers dashed between parked cars, and Jake staggered to his feet and chased after them.

Peter caught Laura in his arms and stared wildly at her. "Are you all right? I'll strangle those stupid morons!" With a grimace, he bit off even angrier words.

"I'm okay," muttered Laura, massaging her sore shoulder. She looked past Peter to see Cupidity lifting her bow with an arrow nocked and ready. The petite archer swiveled slowly as she followed a moving target in the parking lot, then she let her missile fly into the darkness.

"No!" shouted Laura a second too late. A distant figure whimpered and sprawled on the ground, but it was hard to see if the arrow had struck her or if she had just tripped.

"What are you doing?" demanded Peter, whirling on Cupidity. "Okay, what they did was bad, but you can't shoot *arrows* at them! You'll get arrested—we'll *all* get arrested."

Cupidity studied Peter as if seeing him for the first time. "You'll do," she said, nodding. Then she nocked another arrow to her bow, drew back the string, and shot Peter at point-blank range.

"No!" cried Laura once again. She rushed forward, but an invisible shock wave slammed into her, sending her reeling back on her heels. With a gasp, Laura felt her legs weaken beneath her, and she tumbled into the mud.

Five

I'm having a really awful nightmare, thought Laura from the hazy depths of a brain fog, *because there's Megan sobbing over Peter's bloody body. No, he's not really covered in blood, unless blood is neon green.*

Laura vaguely remembered something about paint and a battle. She had been involved too, because her shoulder hurt and there was purple paint on her face and glasses. Jake was yelling and stomping around, and a couple of people had gathered to watch the spectacle.

What a stupid dream, she thought.

"Oh, my precious! Oh, Peter!" wailed Megan, who in this dream was dressed like a soldier. The cheerleader bent over the red-haired, paint-covered boy and shook him as if trying to bring him back from the dead. "I didn't mean to hurt you! I would *never* hurt you!"

"What are you talking about?" demanded Jake, who was also in this dream. He shook his fists at both Megan and Chelsea. "You shot paintballs at us! You totally meant to hurt us. You're psychos!"

"Well, she shot arrows at us!" exclaimed Chelsea, pointing an accusatory finger at Cupidity.

Cupidity smiled innocently beneath several coats of contrasting paint, and she pointed to her multicolored hair. "Do I look like I started this? And look what you did to my car! I ought to have you arrested for that alone."

Now Laura stirred from her stupor, because something had a hint of reality. *Of course, reality is often mixed up in dreams,* she told herself. *Look, there's Megan kissing the paint off Peter's face while sobbing pathetically. They're both real people, yet this would never happen in real life.*

Laura relaxed, knowing she was still in

a dream. A stranger, someone who seemed to work in this park place, stepped forward and said, "Okay, do you want me to call the police? What about an ambulance for them?"

He pointed to Peter, who had Megan draped all over him, sobbing fitfully. Suddenly Peter reached up and grabbed her butt.

"Well, I think he's still alive," said Cupidity.

"Hey, that's *my* girlfriend!" snapped Jake.

"Megan . . . Megan!" breathed Peter. He opened his eyes and saw Megan only inches away. From the grin that spread across his face, it looked as if Peter had died and gone to heaven. Sobbing for joy, they embraced.

Laura giggled dazedly. *What a crazy dream.*

"Teenagers!" growled the old stranger, waving his hand at them. "All of you, get out of here before the sheriff comes by. And you two girls—" He pointed to Megan and Chelsea. "Don't ever come back."

Megan was oblivious to anything but Peter Yarmench, and she grunted as she helped him to his feet. They were instantly besieged by Jake and Chelsea, who didn't look very happy.

Laura felt strong hands under her armpits, and she turned to see Cupidity deftly lifting her to her feet. In doing so, Cupidity smeared paint all over Laura's back, and it felt cold and sticky in the night air.

"Don't wake me up," muttered Laura. "I'm having a weird dream."

Cupidity laughed. "Come on, Sleeping Beauty, let's get out of here before the old man calls the cops." She peered across the parking lot and called, "Jake!"

Jake was pointing his finger and yelling at Megan and Peter. After a few moments, Chelsea joined in, shrieking at her best friend, but the cheerleader and the gangly geek were lost in each other's embrace. They looked like drowning victims cling-ing to life preservers.

As the small crowd drifted away, Jake walked back over to Laura and Cupidity shaking his head. "Dude, I don't get it. She hit him with a couple of paintballs, and now he's like her long-lost love."

"Don't worry," said Laura blissfully, "it's all a dream, it's not real."

Jake stared at her. "Hello! Get a grip, will you? Your date just ditched *you* for *my* girlfriend!"

"I thought you and Megan were over," said Cupidity, folding her arms. "What's the deal, Jake?"

"Hey, it's just a shock, that's all," he answered, turning away from them. When he caught sight of Peter and Megan again, he scowled.

Laura smiled at Jake's discomfort until she saw Chelsea headed their way. The curvy, dark-haired beauty looked frumpy in her army fatigues, and she pouted under her bulky mask. "Can I get a ride with you guys?" she pleaded. "Those two lovebirds don't even know I exist."

"It's just a dream," answered Laura confidently. "Don't sweat it."

"It's no dream," said Cupidity gravely. "Peter and Megan have found each other, and we should be happy for them. Wake up and smell the love connection." She reached out and pinched Laura's arm.

"Ow!" exclaimed Laura, as everything

came into focus. Jake Mattson was standing before her, looking miserable. In the distance, Jake's longtime girlfriend, Megan, was making out with the unlikely Peter Yarmench. And Chelsea's stunned, crestfallen expression only verified this bizarre turn of events. The only person who looked contented was Cupidity. But then again, she barely knew these people.

Memories suddenly flooded back, and Laura stammered, "D-did you shoot Peter with an arrow?"

Cupidity laughed. "Does he look like he's been shot with an arrow? I told you, I use my bow symbolically, so I don't really get angry with people. It's working, isn't it?" she asked as she flipped her paint-covered hair. "I got the worst of this prank, and I'm not angry. So the rest of you, chill out."

"Chill out?" said Jake in confusion. "You must've gotten hit in the head by those stupid paintballs. That's a cheerleader over there with the king of the dorks!"

"Hey!" said Laura angrily, "Peter is my friend."

Chelsea broke into tears and sobbed

pitifully as she climbed out of her paintball gear, which she had worn over her regular clothes. "What's going on? First Cody leaves me, and now I lose my best friend! This is so unfair!"

"Cheer up!" chirped Cupidity, clapping her hands together like a cheerleader. "It's a school night, and we'll all get home in time to make our parents happy. Who cares if we have a little paint on us?"

Chelsea sniffed and grabbed the new girl's paint-smeared arm. "I'm sorry about everything, Cupidity. We followed you here, and it wasn't until we saw that we could rent paintball stuff that we decided to tag you." She looked wistfully over her shoulder. "I didn't think Megan would get so weirded out over it."

"Forget it," insisted Cupidity, happily leading the way to her car. "Get in the car, and don't worry about getting paint on the seats."

"This is why I hate archery," grumbled Jake. He pointed back into the shadows. "Yarmench, I'm not done with you yet!"

No answer came from the funky complex of trees and shooting ranges, and the lights over the paintball field suddenly blinked out, leaving them in deep shadows. One by one, the uniformed figures disappeared into the darkness, and Laura shivered with a feeling of unease.

She wanted to call after Peter and tell him to get back where he belonged, but she had resisted others doing that to her. Peter had found something unusual, and why should she begrudge him that? Maybe Megan was playing him along to get even with Jake, but her concern for Peter had looked genuine. She wasn't that good an actress.

What exactly happened to me? Laura asked herself, but her memories remained vague. Starting with the paintball pummeling, she wasn't sure what she'd experienced, only that something had hit her. *An invisible force?* Or maybe it was just the splatter of a paintball. One thing was certain—this wasn't her typical Tuesday night.

When Laura reached the car, Chelsea was in the back seat, still babbling and crying. "I can't believe it! This is totally whack. Jake, what will we do for the Homecoming Dance? If I don't go with Cody, and you don't go with Megan . . . well, that makes everything totally whacked out! Who will be the king and queen?"

Laura had to resist rolling her eyes as she got in the car next to Chelsea.

"When is this dance?" asked Cupidity with another flip of her paint-splattered hair.

"It's a formal. Early in October," whined Chelsea. "Like three weeks from now."

"Who cares?" muttered Jake. He pounded a beefy fist into his palm. "That geek is going to have some explaining to do."

Laura looked over her shoulder, searching the parking lot for Peter. It was just sinking in that her date had been taken away by the future Homecoming Queen, and she was going home without even getting a kiss. Not that she necessarily *wanted* one from Peter, but still. This was a terrible first date!

Cupidity hummed as she started the car engine. When she moved in her paint-covered clothes, she made squishy sounds on the seat. "Ah, it felt good to shoot again," she remarked.

"What are you talking about?" said Jake, who stared in amazement at his cheerful date. "Tonight was a bust."

"Depends on how you look at it," answered Cupidity. "For example, you'll never have to worry about Megan bugging you again." She laughed softly as Jake scowled.

Laura glanced over her shoulder again, but Peter was gone.

"How could she turn Peter into a love zombie?" asked Taryn with a disdainful sniff. She and Laura were standing at the back of the lunch line, watching Peter Yarmench and Megan Rawlins near the front of the line. The moonstruck couple were gazing at each other so intently that the line had stopped moving. In one day, Peter and Megan had become one of those insufferable, inseparable couples who cling to each other all day long. Finally somebody yelled at them, and they moved a few steps, still gazing at each other with goo-goo eyes.

"You were there—what happened?" asked Taryn.

Laura shook her head. "I was there, but

I have no idea what happened. Megan hit him with a couple of paintballs, and he passed out. She felt really bad about it, and then she was thrilled when he woke up. They've been like this ever since."

"Ew!" exclaimed Taryn, wrinkling her nose. "Whoever thought getting hit by paintballs could be so romantic?"

"Yep." Laura nodded glumly and looked around the crowded cafeteria. She was trying to find Cupidity, who had disappeared shortly after they arrived at school that morning. Last night had been a blur, and now that Laura was clear-headed, she had questions for the new girl.

She found Taryn staring at her with pity. "What?" asked Laura.

"It's just that . . . you go on a date for the first time in like forever, and you lose your date to Megan Rawlins," said Taryn. "That's raw. What are you going to do about it?"

"Do about it?" snapped Laura. "Do you want me to steal him away from Megan? Look at them! I've never seen Peter look at anything like that . . . except maybe pepperoni pizza."

Taryn lowered her voice to add, "They say that Jake Mattson is going to do something about it after school."

"Where did you hear that?"

"Oh, just around." Taryn smiled slyly. "So, will there be any more double dates with Cupidity?"

"I don't know if I can stand the excitement," admitted Laura. "Look, I have to find her. I don't want Peter to get hurt. Catch you later." She rushed out of the lunch line, accepting the fact that she wouldn't get anything to eat.

Laura prowled the cafeteria, then wandered the halls, looking for Cupidity. She finally decided to check outside in the parking lot. Although students weren't allowed to leave campus during lunch, Cupidity tended to follow her own rules.

She finally found her new friend sitting on the hood of her convertible, which was sparkling clean again. Cupidity was talking to an unlikely person, Emma Langdon, and the goth leader with the spiky black hair was nodding at something she said. Emma handed Cupidity a piece of paper, and they both studied it for a moment.

When Laura approached, Emma tucked the paper back in her jacket and gave the valedictorian a smirk.

"I heard you had quite a date last night," Emma said.

"Yeah," answered Laura, "it was more fun shooting at the targets than *being* the targets."

"Man, if I were you, I would so get even with them!" vowed Emma, pounding her fist into her palm. "Those snots think they can get away with anything, and now Megan has ripped off a new boyfriend from the brainiac bunch."

"Yeah," answered Laura, bowing her head and wanting to change the subject. "What else were you two talking about?"

"The usual," answered Cupidity. "Boys."

Emma blushed behind her mask of heavy eye shadow and pale foundation and pointed toward Cupidity. "You'll keep it quiet, right?"

"Don't worry," said Cupidity. "I have great respect for love and secrets. Let me handle it."

Emma glanced at Laura and muttered, "Your friend's okay. Sorry everyone's on your case about her. See ya." With a wave, Emma swaggered across the parking lot as if she owned it.

"You know, I kind of like her," said Cupidity. "She reminds me of my mother—smoldering and intense."

"Where have you been hiding all morning?" asked Laura, wringing her hands. She was nervous for Peter's safety, but she didn't want to jump in about that and look like she was freaking out.

Cupidity admired her reflection in her windshield. "After I dropped you off, I left."

"What? You ditched all your morning classes?" asked Laura in amazement.

"Well, I had to get my car cleaned," answered Cupidity, affectionately slapping the hood of her prized vehicle.

"But your parents—" Laura bit her lip, because she remembered that Cupidity was self-sufficient, no untidy parents around. Although she looked young and fresh, who could tell for sure that she was a high school student? Maybe she was a cop or a con artist or something.

"I'm getting paranoid," blurted Laura.

Cupidity shrugged and patted her on the back. "Well, it comes with the territory. You should have thought of that before—" The blond girl stopped in mid-sentence and started searching through her purse. "What did I do with my cell phone? I hate those things."

"Before what?" demanded Laura, certain she was going to say more.

"Totally nothing," replied Cupidity with a flip of her hair. "Emma was showing me a photo of a boy she likes, as if I didn't know. She wants me to arrange a double date for *her*—can you believe? But I don't think that guy is right for her. She needs to get out of her rut."

"Like Peter did?" asked Laura, wringing her hands again. "What's happening? My life has been turned upside down, and I don't know what happened. Everything seems so crazy . . . ever since I've been hanging out with you."

"Don't blame all your problems on *me*," responded Cupidity with a sniff. "If you liked Peter, why didn't you grab him? You had plenty of opportunity."

Laura's shoulders slumped. She thought

about denying it, but she had a feeling her friend was dead on. "Yeah, you're right," she muttered, "I'm hopeless with boys. But at least I'm not the only one who's confused. I mean, who would have thought Megan Rawlins even knew Peter was alive?"

"Maybe Megan has always liked him," answered Cupidity with a shrug, "and when he got hurt, something snapped in her brain. Love is crazy like that. Okay, so we've crossed off Peter and Jake. Now, who do you *really* like? Cody?"

"Oh, I don't know anymore," said Laura in exasperation. "One thing for sure, I don't want to see Jake do something to hurt Peter. Have you heard the rumors? Can you reason with that Neanderthal?"

"Did you ever try to reason with a Neanderthal?" asked Cupidity with a chuckle. "Never mind. If it gets out of hand, I'll deal with him. Come on, let's try to find him."

The halls were crowded with kids rushing to class after lunch, or rushing to the next lunch period. Laura and Cupidity searched until they were both late, but they didn't find Jake. Several of his friends claimed not to have seen him, and it looked as if he was trying to avoid Cupidity at all costs.

The afternoon crawled by, and Laura could only stare at the clock and feel helpless. *We won't be able to find Jake before he finds Peter,* she thought with dread. *And how could we stop him, anyway?*

When the final bell rang and the kids stampeded into the hallways, there was a feeling of electricity in the air. Someone had stolen Jake Mattson's girlfriend, and it was way too weird a someone to just let it go. It was causing ripples in the smooth pools of high school status.

Laura got caught up in the flow of the crowd heading out of the building, all of them looking for Jake or the love zombies, Megan and Peter. Laura also searched for Cupidity, with no luck, but she managed to hook up with Taryn and a few other friends.

A crowd was gathering at the far corner of the school parking lot, and Laura sprinted ahead of Taryn and Ashley to see what was going on. A group of students had surrounded Megan and Peter, pestering them with questions about their new-found love. The happy couple, meanwhile, seemed lost in their own world, content to just gaze into each other's eyes.

The group parted as Jake muscled through to join in the questioning. He shrugged off two of his friends who were trying to stop him, because they knew how jealous Jake could be. Apparently, so did Megan, who clung to Peter for support. Laura could see fire in Peter's green eyes—she knew he would defend himself and Megan. But it didn't make her feel much better.

The crowd had taken a few steps away from Laura, too, and she realized that she stood apart. Most of the students had heard about what happened the night before, so they expected some kind of reaction from her, too. *I'm the other wronged party,* she thought with a sinking feeling. *At least that's what they all think.*

"How long has this been going on?" yelled Jake. "Have you two been fooling around behind my back?"

"Of course not," said Peter, trying to sound calm. But then he took his hand from Megan's waist and balled it into a fist. "You know, you dumped her, remember."

Jake puffed out his chest beneath his tight polo shirt. "Are you kidding? That wasn't serious—how can I be serious about Cupidity? It was just a misunderstanding between me and Megan, and you jumped in like the loser you are!"

"He's not a loser," countered Megan. "He's wonderful! *You're* the loser!"

Jake roared and took another step closer, fists flailing. But Megan stood her ground and bravely warded off the attack. Jake tried to reach around her, but she blocked his every move; the best he could do was to give Peter a symbolic shove and back off. Peter staggered but stayed on his feet.

Now the crowd was into it, egging them on. Laura couldn't get over how ridiculous the whole scene was. And she finally ran into the middle, the mob roaring their approval. "Hey, I was there last night too!" she yelled at Jake. "Peter was *my* date, so I got dumped the same as you." Then, realizing how pathetic that sounded, she took a deep breath. "Look, you were clearly with Cupidity last night, so stop whining about it."

Jake scowled. "Your friend Cupidity is a skank, a tease . . . and a nutcase on top of it!" The crowd tittered with uneasy laughter at this Jerry Springer moment.

Suddenly the group shifted, and a dazed-looking Emma Langdon muscled her way through. She looked like a person dying of thirst who has suddenly seen a lake. "Jake!" she croaked, holding out a trembling hand.

Along with everyone else, Laura was watching Emma's dramatic entrance, but she still caught a flash of reflected light in the corner of her eye. Someone grunted, and she whirled around to see Jake stagger forward, as a gust of wind pushed her back a step. The preppy king swayed to and fro and looked as if he would pass out, but Emma Langdon rushed in to catch him.

From back near the school building, a loud authoritative voice boomed, "What's going on over there? Break it up now."

Everyone realized that the show was over and scattered quickly toward their cars. Taryn tugged on Laura's sleeve and urged her to move, but she had to hang back for a moment. She could see Emma kneeling beside a dazed Jake Mattson, comforting him. *What happened to him?* wondered Laura. She hadn't seen anything hit him, only that vague flash, but maybe Megan had struck him from behind.

The vice principal was bounding across the lot toward the disbanding group, and Taryn pulled harder on her sleeve. "Come on!"

Laura let Taryn lead her away, just as Cupidity's car shot by, tires squealing. As the rear end fishtailed, the yellow convertible made a sensational U-turn to stop right next to Jake and Emma. Cupidity waved them into her car and sped away while the vice principal yelled.

Students were piling into cars and zooming off in different directions, and Laura had no time to think about what had just happened. When she reached the sidewalk, she saw Megan and Peter in the distance, strolling hand in hand as if nothing had happened. They looked blissful, not even mortified by the fact that they didn't have a car. Laura slowed down and shook her head, thinking that Megan probably hadn't walked home since grade school.

Why do I care so much? she thought. *Could I actually be jealous?* The happy couple definitely grated on Laura. She could understand how Peter deserved some good luck in love, but Megan Rawlins? The cheerleader *always* had good luck. Still, being around Peter made her seem more normal, more mellow, almost fading into the background at times. Megan had given up ruling the popular crowd in order to obsess on Peter, which was an improvement, she guessed.

Laura turned to look for Taryn and spotted her trailing by several strides. "I'll see you later!" she called. "I've got to talk to someone."

Six

Greasy smoke from the barbecue wafted through the back patio of the Mount Olympus Retirement Home. While most of the gods and goddesses lounged by the pool, sipping nectar, three of them stood in the shadows of the patio. They gazed solemnly at a shallow bowl made from the finest black porcelain. Filled with water, it stood on a pedestal, and smoke seemed to gather around the gaunt figures of Mercury, Jupiter, and Vulcan.

Mercury stood to the king's right, but Vulcan shook his bushy head and limped away from the pedestal. "I don't see a darn thing."

"Give it a minute," said Mercury. "It's a miratorium, not a TV."

"There!" croaked Jupiter, pointing into the bowl. In the flickering glow of the bug zappers, Jupiter and Mercury stared at the shimmering portal of blackness.

After a moment, Mercury saw Cupid, in his sultry guise of young maiden, shoot his magical bow in an evening encounter and again in a large parking lot during the day. The elder god felt an emotional tug on his immortal heart, and he could sense the undying love of the two couples Cupid had united. However, he knew from the shimmering vision in the bowl that Laura Sweeney remained unfulfilled.

"*Twice* he has used his powers," remarked Jupiter with a frown on his droopy face.

"Twice?" asked Vulcan curiously.

"But not to aid Laura Sweeney," added Mercury.

Vulcan scowled. "Ack, what is that irresponsible imp doing? I swear, that boy can't be given the simplest task. Those high school students don't need Cupid—they have raging hormones!"

"Maybe you made his disguise too good," remarked Mercury with a disdainful raised eyebrow. "Looking like he does, that cherub could be having too much fun."

Jupiter lowered his bushy eyebrows at the messenger god. "Merc, do you know what I'm thinking?"

The god looked down at his winged slippers and sighed. "You want me to go to Ohio to check up on him . . . or her. What about asking for help from Venus?"

"No!" shouted Vulcan and Jupiter at the same time, and they glanced at one another with suspicion.

"If we alert Venus, the cure could be worse than the bite," said Jupiter. "And perhaps we're worried about nothing. All I'm asking you to do, Brother, is take a firsthand look at the situation."

"Will you need a disguise?" asked Vulcan. "Perhaps you could be a dog? Kids like them."

Mercury gave him an imperious scowl. "A dog? I think not. Besides, I couldn't disguise myself from Cupid—he's too clever. But I will have to assume an identity that will get me close to him. Perhaps you could take a few centuries off my face."

"Heh, heh!" laughed Vulcan with a wheeze. "You won't look a day over sixty."

Laura tiptoed down the sidewalk, trying not to make any noise as she snuck up on Peter and Megan, who were talking in a low, intimate whisper. She wanted to make it look as if she had just stumbled on them, not that she was following them. From Peter, she wanted to find out how it felt to fall madly in love, and why she couldn't bring herself to do it. From Megan, she wanted to know how she could throw away twelve years of class consciousness in one brave kiss.

Secretly, Laura also wanted to make sure Megan was genuine and that she wasn't pulling the ultimate punk on Peter. Even thinking about such a prospect made her furious, and Laura gritted her teeth as she strode forward. Lost in imagined anger, she accidentally tripped over a crack in the sidewalk and stumbled forward, plowing into Megan's back.

"Hey!" shouted the shapely girl, whirling around with fists raised. "You want a piece of me too?"

"Whoa!" said Laura, jumping back, trying to wipe the envy and anger off her face. "I didn't mean anything—I just fell forward. I was the one stopping the stupid fight, remember?"

Megan dropped her hands a little, but she still looked suspicious.

Laura glanced from Peter to Megan and twisted her hands as she said, "Look, other people are being weird, but I'm not trying to be. I mean, I don't care that you two are together. Peter, I'm *glad* you've got a girlfriend . . . even if it's not someone I would ever guess."

"What's that supposed to mean?" asked Megan, lifting her fists again. Laura recoiled a few more steps, because she could see how Megan's possessive side had probably driven Jake crazy. It didn't seem to have the same effect on Peter . . . yet.

In fact, Peter took in the whole awkward exchange with a dimwitted smile. "Hey, you two, there's no point in anyone fighting. They'll all get used to us being together. They'll *have* to." With that, he threw a gangly arm around Megan and pulled her close to him.

At the overt show of affection, Megan gave Laura a triumphant sneer. "Yeah, they'll have to get used to us being together, whether they like it or not. Any other questions, Laura?"

About a thousand, she thought, stunned. But she could only manage to blurt, "When did you two . . . when did you realize you were in love?"

That question brought puzzled expressions to both of their faces, and the love zombies looked curiously at each other. "Well, I always thought Megan was the hottest, the coolest, the most—"

"Okay, I get the picture," replied Laura, cutting him off. "What about you, Megan? When did you know?"

The dark-haired beauty shook her head as if it was an incredibly stupid question. "I guess . . . I have always liked him. Yeah, that's it—from the time I was in kindergarten, I liked Peter!"

"Then how come you never talked to him before our date last night?" asked Laura sweetly.

Megan bristled once again. "Hey, that's none of your business, and I don't even think it's true." She turned and batted her eyelashes at her beloved. "Sweetie, I must have talked to you lots of times before that night . . . didn't I?"

Peter scrunched his face, thinking hard. He finally smiled and said, "Yes, you asked me for a pencil once in fifth grade."

"No, seriously," said Megan, looking troubled. "I feel as if I've always loved you, but I was afraid to express it. Then when I saw you lying there . . . in the mud and the paint, knowing that *I* put you there . . . my heartstrings just snapped."

Laura nodded with understanding, because she had actually seen that happen. Peter had looked pretty pathetic, but there was still something wrong with this picture.

"I don't think *you* knocked him out," said Laura with a frown. "I can't remember exactly what happened, but Cupidity did hit you with an arrow, didn't she?"

"Right!" Megan snorted sarcastically. "That cow couldn't hit the broad side of the principal with her stupid bow. I tripped over something, or somebody pushed me— I can't remember."

"Hey, I think we all hit our heads out there," said Peter, "so what does it matter? It was a dumb stunt, but it worked out great—for us." He gave Megan another insufferable hug.

"Sweetie, it wasn't a dumb stunt," protested Megan softly, staring up at Peter with puppy-dog eyes. "It started out really funny, and I thought we improvised it like champs. We totally didn't know what we were going to do to Jake and Stupidity. Excuse me, Cupidity."

Laura opened her mouth to defend her absent friend, but she really couldn't think of any reason to absolve Cupidity. She had shot an arrow at Megan and pointed one at Peter. Clearly neither one of them had holes in them, but they were stupid in love. *Cupidity and stupidity,* she thought, *they do seem to go together.*

She looked somberly at Peter and said from her heart, "I feel like I'm missing something here, but I'm happy that you're happy. You've got to be better for Megan than that jerk Jake could ever be, and I hope she appreciates you."

Megan sneered. "What I'd appreciate,

Laura, is if you left us alone. I know he used to be one of your friends, but now he's all mine."

"Hey, babe, that's a little harsh, isn't it?" asked Peter. "I didn't agree to give up all my friends for you."

Megan put her hands on her hips and stared at him. "Come on, you hardly *have* any friends. I've got enough friends for both of us, so you don't need this loser."

"I'm glad to see you haven't changed all that much," cracked Laura as she turned and strode away.

She got only a few steps down the sidewalk before Peter caught up to her and grabbed her arm. "Laura, please!" he begged. "Stop and talk to me! She didn't mean it."

Laura stopped long enough to look back at Megan, whose eyes were shooting laser beams at her. "She meant it," hissed Laura. "But maybe she's right. Maybe she *is* all you need. Why would you need me or any of your old friends if you have the Homecoming Queen?" She yanked her arm out of his grip and dashed down the sidewalk.

"Laura!" Peter called after her, his voice filled with confusion and guilt. But Laura didn't stop again. She didn't want him to see her crying.

Laura's run eventually mellowed into a walk, and she called her parents to say she would be late. It was unusually cool for an early autumn afternoon, and she kept going for miles, letting the cool bracing air shake her into reality. She hated to admit it, but even Megan was right—she had to accept what had happened even if she couldn't explain it. And Peter was still Peter—though clearly a bizarre in-love version of himself.

Laura sniffed glumly but held her head up as she walked. One good thing had come from talking to Megan—she realized that the girl hadn't changed. If anything, being in love with Peter had made her more nasty and controlling than before, only now it was directed at one person instead of her hand-picked group. It was Megan and Peter in a very exclusive club: them against the whole school. *Maybe love doesn't turn you into a different person or a better person,* she decided, *just a more obsessed person.*

Laura scowled, because outside of their classes she knew she'd never see Peter alone anymore. *But why do I want to see Peter at all?* she asked herself. *I never thought about him like this before Megan came along. Cupidity is right—there are lots of other boys out there. I can certainly find one of my own. After all, love is in the air.*

Though she was walking a roundabout route, Laura realized she was heading toward Cupidity's apartment. She was going to ask the new girl for advice and find out what she had seen in the parking lot or heard from Emma and Jake in the car. Maybe Emma had told Cupidity what had freaked her out so much during the fight. It was truly amazing that Cupidity had rescued Jake like that after all the unkind things he said about her, but she was a big-hearted person.

The more Laura thought about it, the more she realized that Emma and Jake must have been freaked out at the same time—maybe by the same thing. They had not really been *together* after the fight, they were just frozen in the same spot. Laura laughed at herself for thinking the pair could ever have been together in any other way.

As she rounded the high wall of hedges that separated the sidewalk from Cupidity's apartment complex, Laura heard giggling. It wasn't little kids, because one of them had a very deep voice. Then she heard the unmistakable clatter of a skateboard, and she realized it was just skaters, probably middle schoolers. She kept walking and turned the corner to approach the guardhouse, where there was actually a guard. For Denton, Ohio, these were very swank apartments.

Suddenly she heard a cry of alarm, and a skateboard shot across her path. It rumbled across the road and skittered to a stop against the curb, as a car had to squeal its brakes to keep from hitting it. "Oh, you silly!" cried a voice. "That's not how you do it!"

A darkly dressed figure with pale skin skipped across the driveway and retrieved the skateboard, while the driver looked on with annoyance. Laughing, smiling—even giggling!—Emma Langdon grabbed the board and rushed back to her friend, who Laura was shocked to see was Jake Mattson.

"Let me try it again," said Jake, taking the board from her. "What do you call that move you do? An ollie?"

Emma giggled again. "First, dude, you've just got to learn to keep your balance. Maybe you're a goofy foot—try leading with your left foot."

"Emma?" asked Laura with amazement. "Jake?"

"Hi!" called Emma. They both smiled at Laura as if the goth chick giving the preppy king a boarding lesson was the most natural thing on earth. "Okay, Jake, try it again with your left foot, more perpendicular to the board. Hold your hands out to keep your balance."

Jake gamefully leaped on the board and promptly fell off again, but he laughed as he landed in a pile of dirt. "Hey, this is hard! I'll never knock skater dudes again."

"You'd better not," said Emma, giving him a warm smile. "I'm going to get you a skateboard for your birthday. When is that?"

"Not until March," Jake answered sadly.

"Then I'll get you one just for being sweet." Emma unleashed a mushy smile on Jake, and he gazed at his pale gothic princess with a goofy grin.

Laura rubbed her eyes, certain she was seeing things. Before now, these two hadn't simply ignored each other as Peter and Megan had, they'd actively *hated* each other. To see them acting cozy and sharing a skateboarding lesson was even more shocking than seeing Peter and Megan together. Once this became common knowledge in school, all the social classes would be flipped upside down.

Flapping her lips, Laura only managed to stammer, "Is . . . is Cupidity at home?"

"Yeah," said Jake, turning his dazzling blue eyes to Laura. "I apologized to her, and I'd like to apologize to you, too, for acting like a jerk. Not that I *am* a jerk—I just act like one sometimes."

Emma beamed with pride. "That was a wonderful apology, Jakey, and she knows you meant it. Dude, we've got to thank Laura for hooking us up with Cupidity. Both of you have been really cool about *everything,* and Jake and I want to triple-date with you. Don't we, Jakey?"

"Uh-huh." He nodded as if he had heard her, but he was too busy casting love-smitten goo-goo eyes to understand anything but the basics.

"To triple-date, I have to find a boyfriend," Laura reminded them. "I'm apparently the only one who can't find one."

"Maybe you're just looking in the wrong place," said Emma, grabbing Jake and pulling him possessively to her ample side. He almost drooled on her thick eye makeup. "Walk on the wild side," suggested Emma as she hugged her preppy prize, whose polo shirt was now dirty and untucked. "Think outside the box."

Laura wagged her finger at the unusual couple. "You two are so outside the box you're in . . . a tetrahedron."

"We'll find you a date for Homecoming," insisted Jake, and he sounded as if he meant it.

"No, thanks!" answered Laura with dread. "I'm still recovering from the last date you arranged for me. I, uh . . . I'll talk to Cupidity." Laura staggered away, thinking that the world had to be coming to an end.

She could accept that a girl might find Peter attractive, and that it might even be someone as unlikely as Megan Rawlins. But Emma Langdon and Jake Mattson pawing each other? This had really gone beyond the laws of physics, romance, and high school order. *Not that I should care,* thought Laura with a frown. *I don't have any claim on Jake. In fact, I wouldn't want that jerk, but Emma should want him even less.* It didn't matter that Jake was now dishing out apologies like a sensitive New Age guy—he still had acted like such a jerk. Megan hadn't really changed, and neither had he. But *something* had happened to them.

Cupidity . . . bow and arrows. Laura's fevered imagination seized on a ludicrous explanation for these two unlikely romances. Cupidity had shot her arrows that fateful night when Megan and Peter fell for each other. . . .

No, it's too insane to think that Cupidity is some kind of modern-day Cupid, Laura decided. *I've got to keep my imagination in check. It's got to be a coincidence that her name is Cupidity. Come to think of it, it's a wonder there aren't more girls with that name. It's kinda pretty.*

Then again, this thing between Emma and Jake was too far beyond normal to have any earthly explanation. But Cupidity hadn't shown up until it was all over. Or had she?

Laura marched up the steps toward Cupidity's apartment, determined to get some answers. She rang the doorbell, and the blond girl answered it wearing a towel, her hair all wet from the shower. A cell phone was stuck in her ear, and she motioned Laura inside her luxurious apartment without ever stopping her conversation.

"Yes, yes, Cody, I know I owe you a date!" she said with a knowing wink at Laura. "Well, I've found that going out on school nights is not such a hot idea, so why don't we wait until Friday? It's only a couple of nights away. But I won't go with you unless I can double-date with Laura Sweeney. You've got friends who would like her, I'm sure. So find one."

Laura waved her hands, trying to get

out of the double-date trap, but Cupidity ignored her. "Just find somebody by Friday, and we'll hang! Later, Cody."

With a satisfied grin on her face, the blond girl turned off the phone and beamed at her best friend. "It's all set for Friday night—don't make any plans. Hang on a second while I get dressed."

"Wait!" Laura tried to protest the arranged date, but Cupidity rushed off to her bedroom. Laura twiddled her thumbs for a few minutes until Cupidity reappeared in jeans and a T-shirt. Laura marveled at how perfect the fresh-faced girl looked without any makeup.

"Don't worry," insisted Cupidity, "we're going to get you a solid date for the Homecoming Dance. Someone who will make you happy and treat you right."

"And just how are you going to do this?" blurted Laura. "How are you putting these weird couples together? And come to think of it, why?"

"What do you mean?" asked Cupidity with a forced laugh. "People double-date all the time, it's no big deal."

"No, that's not a big deal," agreed

Laura. "But Peter and Megan going together? And now Emma and Jake—that's like the Alien dating the Predator! They couldn't stand to be in the same school before this, and now they're best buddies? It's not natural."

"Love is always natural," insisted Cupidity. "It's just surprising sometimes. Out of all the people I know, I didn't think *you* would complain about people crossing social barriers to go out with each other."

Laura shook her head and tried to corral her scattered thoughts. "I'm not complaining about it—I'm just trying to figure out how it happened! I saw you pick up Jake and Emma in your car after the fight. Are you saying that you had *nothing* to do with their romance?"

Cupidity shrugged. "Well, I gave Emma the same advice I gave you—to get out of your rut. If you can't win at eight ball, switch to nine ball."

"What?" asked Laura, puzzled. "What did you do to . . ."

"What do you think I did to them?" scoffed Cupidity, putting her hands on her slender hips.

Laura's mouth opened, but the ridiculous words froze on her tongue. She couldn't accuse this cute, ditzy new girl of being some kind of relative of Cupid's—the whole idea was absurd. Instead she asked lamely, "How did you get your first name?"

The blond girl shrugged and tried to look disinterested. "What excuse do parents need for crazy names anymore? They wanted something like Felicity or Charity, so they picked Cupidity."

"Have you ever looked up the meaning of cupidity? It means 'greed, desire, wanting something that doesn't belong to you.'"

"And your point?" asked Cupidity, her blue eyes narrowing with anger. "What's your deal, Laura? Do you want to be in love, or don't you? Do you want my help, or do you want to stumble along in the weeds, getting nowhere? Now you've seen that people *can* find love when they open themselves up to it. If they keep themselves all scrunched and uptight, like you, it ain't gonna happen."

Feeling sufficiently sidetracked, Laura sighed. Once again, it had all come back around to her and her deficiencies, which didn't seem quite fair. Whatever she was going through, it didn't explain these two strange romances, which had exploded right after the arrival of the strange new girl.

With a sympathetic grin Cupidity reached out and patted Laura's shoulder. "Don't worry, it'll happen for you. Look, you seem to think I can work some magic, so why not give me a chance to help? Cody's pretty desperate to go out with me; let's see what kind of dude he scrounges up for you. We know he can't go back to Peter, so it's got to be someone different."

Her pleading smile was so sincere that Laura felt herself giving in. "Okay, whatever. But I'm gonna watch Emma and Jake."

"Do that. Maybe you'll learn something," answered Cupidity. "If you see them, tell them they can keep my skateboard. I'm going to bed early."

"That's *your* skateboard?" asked Laura with surprise.

Cupidity shrugged. "When in Rome, do as the Romans. I'll see you tomorrow." The beautiful blond girl sauntered into the living room, where she grabbed a fat cigar from the mantel and calmly lit it. Puffing away, Cupidity disappeared into the kitchen, leaving Laura to show herself out.

Ew, thought Laura with a lump in her stomach, *she smokes cigars! And what does she mean by, "When in Rome do as the Romans"?*

The perplexed teenager stepped into the bracing fall air; it was almost dark, and lights twinkled in the bare trees of the apartment complex. If Emma and Jake were still playing with their skateboard, they were awfully quiet about it. As Laura walked down the sidewalk toward the street, she could hear the echo of another pair of footsteps. She looked up to see a slender, well-dressed man with a cane ambling toward her.

He tipped his homburg hat and gave her a crinkled smile, and she had the feeling that he was very old, and very sweet. His wing-tipped shoes paused in mid-step, and he asked, "Miss, may I bother you for directions?"

"Of course," she answered, happy to help the man.

He looked puzzled as he waved his cane

at the different buildings in the complex. "I'm looking for apartment C-17, but I'm not sure which one—"

"C-17?" said Laura with excitement. "Isn't that where Cupidity lives?"

The old man's face brightened. "Why, do you know Cupidity? You wouldn't by any chance be Laura Sweeney?"

"Yes!" she answered. "But how do you know my name?"

The elder chuckled. "Oh, Cupidity has spoken of you. She says that you've been a very good friend in her new school situation. I must go and surprise her." The old man shuffled off.

"Excuse me," said Laura, "who . . . who are you?"

"Oh, I'm Cupidity's father," he answered with another crinkled grin. "It's been some time since I've seen her."

Laura stepped forward and lowered her voice. "Listen, you may smell cigar smoke in her apartment, but that wasn't her. It was the . . . dishwasher repairman."

The elder's smile looked pained as he replied, "I know Cupidity smokes cigars. That's one bad habit we'll be sure to break.

Anything else I should know about my lovely daughter?"

For a moment Laura considered telling him about the bow and arrows at school, but decided against it. Instead she chirped, "She's, uh . . . she's quite a girl."

"Yes," answered the old man doubtfully. "A girl . . . to warm any father's heart. Thank you for your help, Laura. I'm sure we'll see you again soon." He tipped his hat and ambled down the sidewalk, relying on his cane.

He must've been about fifty years old when she was born, thought Laura, but she wiped that thought out of her mind. *So Cupidity has a real father,* she mused. *That rules out any crazy idea about her being Cupid's evil spawn.*

With a sigh Laura hurried into the street and down the sidewalk, anxious to get home in time for dinner.

Seven

The next morning Laura lingered in bed, not really wanting to go to school, which was unusual for her. After her mother had to call her three times to get up, Mom sweetened the deal by telling Laura that she could take the car. Knowing she would be driving herself and not depending on Cupidity for a ride was enough to get Laura crawling out of bed.

Still Laura moved so slowly that she was nearly late to school. Pulling the white grandma-style sedan into the parking lot, she grabbed her books and dashed toward the main doors. She thought she had avoided most of the gossip and hoopla, but then Taryn ambushed her right inside.

"Did you hear? Did anyone tell you?!" she shrieked as she grabbed Laura's arm. "Emma and Jake are . . . together!"

"I know," muttered Laura.

"Like *together* together. They're holding hands!" exclaimed Taryn.

"I heard they exchanged notes!" whispered Ashley, who grabbed Laura's other arm. "In the middle of the hallway!"

"I know, I know," repeated Laura as she tried to muscle her way through her friends. The whole corridor was abuzz.

Taryn shook her head and grumbled, "Jake's gotta be punkin' her out. It's a goof."

"No goof," answered Laura. "Think back, Taryn. I told you about this on the phone yesterday. It was after the fight."

"Crazy!" blurted Taryn. "You did! You're like . . . psychic!"

Ashley frowned in worry. "You know, my dad says they're putting too much fluoride in the water. Maybe it's causing us all to go crazy."

Laura sighed. "Tell your dad to give me a web address—I'm looking for an explanation." She charged ahead and ran into a muscular body looming in her path. He was dressed in really baggy pants and had multiple bandannas tied to his bag and his clothes. "Oh, sorry, Chester!" said Laura with a gulp.

Chester was one of the toughest guys in the school, but he jumped back in embarrassment and looked past her. "Excuse me. Uh, Taryn, can I talk to you?"

"Sure, Chester," she answered, walking up to the looming presence, a curious look on her face. "You have chemistry before I do, so the test is whatever—"

"It's not about chemistry," he replied, gazing down at her with extreme earnestness. "It's about the Homecoming Dance."

Whoa! thought Laura. *Where did that come from?* Before she could hear more, Ashley grabbed her arm and dragged her away.

"Did you hear that?" she whispered. "Chester is asking Taryn to Homecoming. I *know* it's the fluoride!"

"No," answered Laura in a daze. "It's just the end of high school as we know it."

The warning bell went off, and the crowd in the hallway began to dissipate.

On instinct, Laura wanted to hang back to see what was happening with Taryn. But she knew that it was a Homecoming invite, and she didn't want to get in the way— even if it was from as unlikely a source as Chester. Still, she thought curiously, she could chalk up one more unlikely match in this romantic dimensional distortion they were all suffering at Fimbrey High.

Before third period Laura met up with Cupidity outside biology class. The new girl looked a bit subdued and was dressed more demurely than usual; her belly button hardly showed at all, as befitted a teenager who had an actual parent at home. "Hey, I met your dad last night," said Laura. "You didn't tell me he was visiting you."

"Yeah," grumbled Cupidity. "I didn't know he was going to pop up. Quite a kidder, my dad—always likes a surprise. Look, we've got to get you fixed up. Have you seen Cody today?"

"I don't exactly travel in Cody's circle," admitted Laura with a puzzled expression. "But I usually see him by now, and I haven't."

"I think he cut school today," muttered

Cupidity. "He probably heard about Jake and Emma, and he didn't want the competition for attention. I didn't know Emma and Jake would turn out to be such a high profile pairing."

Laura nodded sagely, while she tried to figure Cupidity out. "Yes, they sorta took the spotlight off Peter and Megan, who are even weirder if you think about it. Before you got involved in these people's lives, you didn't know them very well."

"Hey, I didn't make any of these people what they are," said Cupidity, sounding defensive. "Jake drooled on me before I pushed a single button—he can act like such a sleaze. Emma Langdon is tough enough to actually stand up to that big head of his. Maybe it will work out."

"Yeah, okay," admitted Laura, bowing her head. "They did look pretty happy together when I saw them yesterday."

Cupidity winked at her, suddenly full of the old spirit. "Don't worry so much. You just be ready for our double date tomorrow night."

Laura tried not to shiver, although another double date sounded more like a threat than a good time. Somehow she summoned the courage to smile and say with a sigh, "I'll be there."

By lunchtime Laura was moping through the hallways, trying to ignore the gossip and the buzz. Were two people falling for each other really worth all this excitement? The fact that it was Jake Mattson had a lot to do with it. She couldn't wrap her brain around any more surprises or unusual romances, so Laura tried not to talk to anyone. As she climbed down the central staircase, headed to her locker, she didn't realize someone was walking beside her until he spoke.

"I've got to talk to you," he said.

Laura lurched to a stop and stared at Peter Yarmench. He immediately bolted two steps ahead of her, as if he feared she would escape to the bottom floor. She could still turn around and run back upstairs, but she was too surprised to move.

"Where's your girlfriend?" asked Laura snidely. She instantly regretted her snippety tone, but it was already out.

"I ditched her," whispered Peter with a

smile. "It wasn't easy, but I had a decoy lure her to the computer lab."

"Is that really a healthy relationship," asked Laura, "when you have to sneak around just to talk to an old friend?"

"No, it's not okay," he admitted, casting his troubled eyes downward and showing her a shock of unruly red hair. "I don't really understand this thing with Megan. It's . . . a little scary."

"Yeah, you look scared all right," said Laura, laying on the sarcasm. "She's Miss Popularity—isn't that what you wanted?"

He shook his head and lifted his startled green eyes to peer into hers, and he seemed to beg for understanding. "You know, it's really weird. I like . . . love Megan and all, and I mean, it's great having a girlfriend. But I really miss you. I mean, I miss us hanging around. You know?"

"I don't think Megan misses me," replied Laura. "And you can't be giving me the 'I just want to be friends' speech, because that's all we ever were—friends."

"I know." His shoulders slumped.

"Besides, you've got a girlfriend," she insisted, "and she obviously doesn't want to share you—even with your old friends."

Peter held out his hand and touched her forearm, and a chill flew up Laura's shoulder. It reminded her of the night she was knocked out, the night Peter had woken up in Megan's arms. "I don't want to lose you," he said in a husky voice. "For some weird reason, falling in love with Megan has opened my eyes . . . and made me realize . . . well, how much I need you around."

Laura couldn't speak, there was such a knot in her throat. She didn't realize how badly she had wanted to hear this, but Peter's timing couldn't be worse. "Okay," she blurted, "so break up with Megan!"

"I can't *do* that." He grimaced and balled his hands into fists, as if he was being torn apart by internal conflicts. She felt sympathy for him, but she also hated him at the same time.

"Call me when you can," Laura muttered. "And lose the dramatics—they don't work."

She hurried down the stairs, trying to lose herself in the lunch crowd. *He wants two girlfriends,* she thought angrily. *Peter is*

*just like Jake and Cody and all the rest of
them—just in love with himself!*

After school Mercury sat in Cupidity's yellow convertible, waiting for the cherub-in-disguise to exit the school. He finally spotted her, surrounded by other teenagers, all of them yakking. Who could possibly be listening when they all talked at once? Nevertheless, Mercury was impressed by how many friends Cupidity seemed to have, and there was one handsome lad, dressed in black leather and silver chains, who would have commanded attention among the gods themselves. He even gave Cupidity a kiss on the cheek.

Before Cupidity reached her car, she bid her friends adieu, although several of them stared curiously at her "father." Mercury tipped his hat politely.

Cupidity gave him a smug smile as she climbed into the driver's seat. "See, I told you they all liked me, and I've got everything under control. Seriously, Mercury, you don't have to hang around here." She started the car engine with a loud *vroom*, and the fumes made Mercury wrinkle his nose.

"They've accepted you, but that doesn't mean you've done the job," said the elderly god with a sniff. "So far, you've paired up other mortals, but not Laura Sweeney."

"They were just warm-ups," insisted Cupidity as she backed the sports car out of its parking space. "I told you I was out of practice. Besides, we're talking about two lousy couples. That's nothing for me—in the old days, I'd do two pairs before breakfast."

"I've met Laura Sweeney," said the elder, "and it doesn't seem that it would be difficult to make a match for her."

The young lady laughed. "Ah, you don't know Laura that well. Outside she seems normal, but inside she's a fruit loop."

She motioned to a gang of students who clogged the sidewalk. "Most of them are ruled by their hormones, but Laura still depends on her brain. Makes it very difficult to get just the right match for her. Sure, I could pair her up with anyone— even you—but would she be happy?"

Mercury shrugged. "Who can guarantee a mortal happiness?"

"Hey, I've only had a few days to get to

know her," said the cherub as her car careened around the corner, tires squealing. "You all agreed that I should have some time to get to know her, so let me do my job! Tell Jupiter and those worried old ladies that all will be well. I've planned a double date for tomorrow night, and I'm sure the arrows will be flying."

"Do you have someone picked out for her?" asked Mercury.

"Yes, Cody Kenyon. Maybe you saw him—black leather jacket, spiked hair, Elvis sneer."

"Oh, yes," answered elder with a knowing smile. "I approve."

"Well, good. So leave me the Hades alone!" Cupidity pulled to a stop and looked at the messenger god. "Can I take you to the airport?"

"Why can't I stick around?" asked Mercury, sounding hurt.

"Parents just get in the way." Cupidity stared pointedly at him. "Airport?"

"You just want to be able to smoke cigars again," muttered the god.

"Well, duh!" Cupidity scowled. "Listen, I'll be back at Mount Olympus when the job is done. You won't be missing anything."

"Remember, your disguise doesn't last forever," warned the god.

"I've got two more weeks!" scoffed the beautiful cherub. "I'll be out of here long before that, believe me."

Mercury sat stiffly in his seat. "Well, I was able to go to the office and fill out some paperwork for you. Perhaps you need me."

"That's good they got to see a parent," allowed Cupidity. "But I don't really *need* a parent—I'm three thousand years old! Come on, Merc, I took a couple extra shots as a warm-up, but now I'm ready to get down to business. You can see that everything is fine here."

"Okay, take me to the airport," grumbled Mercury. "We won't watch you or nag you—we'll just trust you."

"Good idea!" chirped Cupidity as the yellow convertible jumped the curb and headed off down the boulevard.

Right behind them came a white sedan driven by a preoccupied Laura Sweeney. "Wasn't that Cupidity's car?" asked Taryn from the passenger seat. "She has the coolest car."

"Huh? Oh, yeah, I guess so," muttered Laura. In truth, she was still so miserable over Peter that she could barely concentrate on driving.

"She had an old guy with her," Taryn pointed out.

"That's her father." Laura brought the car to a stop at the corner and tried to snap out of her daze. "Listen, I'm going to the library. Where am I taking you?"

"To cloud nine," answered Taryn dreamily as she hugged her books to her chest. "Can you believe it? I've got a date for Homecoming!"

"Congratulations," answered Laura, trying to muster a smile. "Chester the Homeboy— who would have thought he was crushing on you?"

"Well, I catch him looking at me a lot in class," answered Taryn, "but I thought he was trying to copy off my paper." She laughed so joyfully that Laura couldn't stay jealous of her old friend's new relationship.

"Are you two going out this weekend?" asked Laura.

Taryn nodded gravely. "Yes, we're going to a rap concert. What do you wear to a rap concert?"

"I'm sure you can wear almost anything. Chester will look out for you."

They drove a bit farther in silence, Taryn gazing wistfully out the window and Laura trying to concentrate on the road. As they turned down the street to Taryn's house, Taryn said, "I know we made fun of Peter and Megan, then Jake and Emma, but I don't think Chester would have asked me out if they hadn't broken the ice."

"Probably not," admitted Laura. "Anarchy in the high school social order is a good thing." She pulled to a stop in front of Taryn's house. "Here you are—cloud nine."

Laura's friend squeezed her arm and looked sympathetically at her. "Don't worry, Laura, we'll get you a date too. Now all the boys in school are up for grabs—not just the ones you're *supposed* to date."

Laura mustered a smile, but that thought wasn't very comforting. Now she could be turned down by *any* guy in school. Taryn jumped out of the car and ran toward her house, no doubt anxious to spread the news about her date. Trying to be happy for her friend, Laura sniffed back her conflicting emotions and waved good-bye as she pulled away from the curb.

Since she had the car, she decided to drive downtown to the big library, where they had all kinds of old and rare books that weren't allowed to be taken out of the building. Laura wasn't sure exactly what she was looking for, just some general research into the supernatural aspects of love. Cupidity might be a regular girl with a regular father, but *some* kind of love bug had infected the kids at Fimbrey. Maybe there was another explanation.

At the library Laura's footsteps echoed down the marble staircase and into the cavernous main chamber. A cold draft swirled around her, and she smelled the musty odor of old paper, fabric, glue, and dust—books. A door creaked somewhere in the old building, and she felt a chill. It almost felt as if these ancient tomes didn't want to give up their secrets. Maybe this was a stupid waste of time, but Laura felt as if she had to do something. It was research or go crazy.

She dove into the card catalog and computer listings and grabbed all the books she could find off the regular shelves. An hour of looking through them didn't really give her anything that she thought was pertinent to the love epidemic.

So Laura culled through the listings of rare and fragile books, which were kept in a special room and not allowed to leave the library. Clutching her requests, she found a librarian, an older woman in a business suit with flaming red hair, and gave her the slips of paper.

"Love spells, love potions, love candles, fortune-telling," said the old librarian, reading the subjects she had requested. When she was finished, the old woman clicked her tongue and gave Laura a sympathetic smile. "You know, dearie, those love spells don't work. Why don't you try the personal ads, like I do."

"Personal ads?" said Laura with a nervous laugh. "I'm a little young for those." She didn't add that the librarian looked a little *old* for personal ads. "I'm really doing this for a school project. If you've got any books about Cupid or Venus, that would be good too. I've read all the mythology books on the shelf."

"Hmmmm," said the librarian, sounding impressed. She gave Laura a wink. "I'll bring you all the good stuff, but they don't have many pictures."

Laura laughed nervously. "That's fine. I don't need pictures . . . I have a good imagination."

"Give me a few minutes." The old woman tottered away, but she didn't return for almost half an hour. Laura had almost given up on her when she finally wheeled in a cart full of books, most of them old and tattered.

"You want the good stuff, right?" she said with a chuckle. "I hope you're not going anywhere for a while."

Laura sighed. "No, I'm not. No place else to go."

Laura Sweeney read and skimmed until the words on the yellowed pages blurred and the windows darkened except for pools of light from the streetlamps. A fierce wind kicked up, and branches scraped against the windows. The history of love, famous lovers, love spats, love spells and potions, and gobs of myths about love spilled from the books. Ghostly love, true love, tragic love, unspoken love, and lots of variations were discussed at length, sometimes with statistics. Laura learned more than she wanted to know about some topics, but she didn't find anything that would explain what was happening to the kids at Fimbrey High.

In all the morass of words and images, there were plenty of stories about Cupid and his mother, Venus. Laura's eyes were drooping as she leafed through one musty volume of Roman mythology, which she had read before. Normally she could lose herself for hours in a book like this, but her energy and hope were waning.

Suddenly Laura's bleary eyes landed on a picture of an old Roman fresco that had been uncovered in the ruins of Pompeii, Italy. The ancient image stopped her cold, and she blinked in amazement at the painting of Cupid and his mother. The youthful cherub wore long blond hair, making his face look an awful lot like Cupidity's. But that wasn't what startled Laura—it was the bow and arrow in his hands. The weapon looked remarkably similar to Cupidity's bow, down to its harp shape and ornate workmanship.

"What the—?" she muttered, rubbing her eyes. "That can't be."

"Did you say something, dearie?" asked the old librarian.

Gripping the book, Laura jumped excitedly to her feet. "Can you make me a photocopy of this page?"

"As long as the pages aren't too brittle," answered the librarian. The old woman grunted when Laura handed her the heavy tome, and she peered at the page with curiosity. "*That's* what you were looking for . . . a picture of Cupid and Venus?"

"It's perfect for what I need," answered Laura with a forced smile. *And that's to discover the truth about Cupidity,* she decided, *which I will do tomorrow night when I get a closer look at her bow. I have to find out whether I'm crazy or the rest of the world is.*

Eight

Smart Cody, thought Laura the moment she opened her front door and saw her date for Friday evening. Cody had enlisted a guy from another high school but of the same tribe as himself—a scruffy, handsome skater dude with spiky, dyed-auburn hair. Laura was reminded of Peter, who had real red hair, but she quickly put that image out of her mind.

"Laura Sweeney, this is my bud Rip Durkens," offered Cody, sounding like the perfect host. Cupidity stood on the step behind her date, looking pleased at his show of good manners. "Rip's a senior, too," added Cody. "He goes to the charter school down at the mall."

"Hi," said the scrawny skater, giving her a wry smile. "I didn't know what to expect, but Cody never steers me wrong." He was charming, especially for someone who was trying to act tough, and Laura was definitely attracted to him.

Down, girl, she told herself. *You have no idea if Rip even wants to be on this date, or how long it's going to last. So just enjoy it for what it is.*

"Cupidity never steers me wrong either," lied Laura, trying to fit in with the theme of the evening. As she stepped out of the house, she yelled back, "Bye! We're leaving now!"

Nobody answered, because her parents were hiding again. The four students walked slowly to the car, and Laura asked, "So what's the plan? Burgers and a movie?" That's what they had talked about earlier, and she hoped it would be a somewhat normal date.

"Burgers, for sure," answered Cody, "then we've got a couple of parties to go to. And maybe we'll end up at Cupidity's place for a private party."

Hmmmm, thought Laura, not certain she

liked the sound of that. "Is your dad home?" she asked Cupidity.

"No," Cupidity answered with a flip of her perfect blond hair. "Daddy Dearest went back to California last night. He just wanted to make sure I was settled in."

Cody laughed appreciatively and turned to his friend. "Rip, can you believe it? Cupidity lives alone. No parents around."

"Niiice," replied Rip, casting a side-long glance at Laura, who tried not to appear too sultry. "Cody and me are going to get a place, as soon as we graduate."

"Shouldn't college or a job come first?" asked Cupidity as they reached her car. Even though the air was getting chilly, she still had the top down.

"Ahh, we'll be on the pro skateboard circuit by then," answered Rip confidently. "You should see us on the half-pipe."

While they talked about their fantastic future, Laura walked to the rear of the car. She felt her back pocket to make sure she still had the picture of Cupid and his bow. "Cupidity," she called. "I've got this heavy purse—do you think I could throw it in your trunk?"

"Sure," Cupidity replied. Pulling a lever under the dashboard, she popped the trunk lid while she made conversation with the boys.

While they were occupied, Laura looked inside the trunk and saw the duffel bag she knew so well. Even though no archery was planned for tonight's date, Cupidity had still brought her bow and arrows with her, which was rather suspicious. Knowing this wasn't the right time to get nosy, Laura dropped her purse into the trunk and shut the lid.

Rip gallantly held the car door open for her with one hand while he pulled the front seat forward with the other. Laura could've jumped into the back seat, but this was nicer. As Laura climbed in, she began to worry about what Cupidity might have planned for them this evening. If she really was a female Cupid, then she was like a god. She could strike without warning, and Laura might find herself crazy in love with a wild skater boy by the end of the night. The prospect of turning into a love zombie, like Peter and Megan, made her shiver.

Suddenly frightened, Laura almost

bolted from the car, but Cupidity started the engine and roared away from the curb, tires squealing. Cody laughed merrily at her reckless driving, and Laura buckled her seat belt. She felt a wiry arm around her shoulder, because Rip was already getting friendly. He didn't even need to be hit by a magic arrow.

"So what are you into?" Rip asked her. "What do you like to do in your spare time?"

"Well," she mused, "I had a job at the Dairy Queen, but I quit that when school started. I like to read."

"Read?" echoed Rip, as if he had never heard of such a thing. "Like what, magazines?"

"Greco-Roman mythology," she answered hesitantly.

Cupidity laughed and said, "Yeah, Laura is really into that stuff—all those silly gods and goddesses."

That remark ticked Laura off, and she decided to give Cupidity a little test. When they stopped at a traffic light, she said, "There are some great love stories in mythology, like Cupid and Psyche. Psyche was the most beautiful woman in the world, and Venus got jealous of her. So she sent her son, Cupid, to make Psyche fall in love with a monster, but instead Cupid fell in love with Psyche. But he was so short and funny-looking that Psyche ran away from him."

"Funny-looking?" scoffed Cupidity. "She never saw him—Cupid was invisible. It was all her stupid sisters!"

Cody gave his date a quizzical stare. "Oh, so you're an expert, too. But look at your name!" He laughed as if he was the first one who had ever made the connection.

Cupidity chuckled uneasily and glanced back at Laura. "I'm no expert . . . but I happen to know that story." As the light changed, she peeled away from the line.

They drove to the Gaslight, a 1950s-style diner where the waitresses wore poodle skirts and beehive wigs. It was a good enough place to get a burger, and Laura ate while Cody and Rip told stories about each other's exploits on skateboards, snowboards, and rollerblades. They were a mutual admiration society, and they were both ready to go pro, by their assessment.

All through dinner, Laura caught Cupidity gazing curiously at her, as if measuring her for an arrow. When Laura mouthed the word "What?" Cupidity shook her head and looked away. Even though her father had left, his visit still seemed to be having an effect on Cupidity. Tonight the new girl seemed uncertain, troubled, and just as real as anyone, and Laura began to feel guilty for thinking such bizarre thoughts about her.

I'm crazy, thought Laura. *She's just trying to do me a favor, and I'm so suspicious of her. How can I be so ungrateful?*

While the boys were laughing at each other's stories, Laura reached over and touched Cupidity's arm. "Hey, cheer up. I'm having a great time. I want to thank you for doing this."

Cupidity brightened. "Are you really? Good, I was beginning to think that it was all for nothing. You *do* want a boyfriend, don't you?"

"Yes, but it's got to be the right one," answered Laura. "Any dude off the street . . . I could do that myself."

"Am I 'any dude off the street'?" asked

Rip with a chuckle. "What are you guys talking about?"

"Blind dates," answered Laura, lifting her glass of soda. "I'm all for blind dates. Here's to blind dates!" She hefted her drink in a toast, and everyone joined her.

"To blind dates!" they echoed.

"And you are not 'any dude off the street,'" Laura told Rip, shooting him what she hoped was a sexy look over the top of her glasses. He seemed appreciative, and he set down his burger to reach for her hand. It was a greasy grip, but Laura didn't yank her hand away. She had to get through this date as gracefully as possible and stop worrying about Cupidity.

After dinner, they jumped back into the convertible and took off, this time with Cody driving. It was so cold in the back seat that Laura welcomed the extra warmth when Rip sat close and put his arm around her. At one point he tried to kiss her, but Cupidity turned around and interrupted them. Laura couldn't tell if that was on purpose or not, but she was too cold to do anything but cuddle with Rip.

After a while they found themselves

cruising the rust-belt outskirts of town, where abandoned factories, rusty grain silos, and run-down warehouses stood. Every window was broken in these dark derelicts of lost industry, and weeds grew on the railroad tracks that ran along the rear of the buildings. This sure wasn't the movies, thought Laura, and she wondered what kind of party could be happening out here in the boondocks.

Only one parking lot in the deserted district had any cars in it, and Cody pulled in there and parked on lumpy, cracked asphalt. With the top down, Laura could hear the muffled thumping of rock music coming from somewhere nearby, but it was drowned out by the chilly wind. She was thankful just to be arriving in civilization where there might be heat, and she almost jumped out of the car before Rip opened the door for her. He held the door like a perfect gentleman, and Cody rushed to do the same for Cupidity.

The guys smiled knowingly at each other, and Laura glanced at her buddy, who gave her a wink. *Cupidity's in charge here,* she told herself, *not these two smug boys.*

"This is a skater rave," explained Cody,

putting his arm around Cupidity's tiny waist. "I think you'll have a good time, but you might have to do some skating."

"Skating?" asked Laura uneasily. "What kind of skating?"

"Skateboard skating," answered Rip as if that explained it all. "It keeps the old people away."

"You'd be surprised at what some old people can do," remarked Cupidity.

"Like what?" asked Cody doubtfully.

She laughed as if remembering something funny. "At this retirement home I know, they race their wheelchairs down the stairs. And they dive off the top floor into the swimming pool."

"Cool," said Cody in admiration. "And where do these crazy old dudes live?"

"In Los Angeles," answered Cupidity. "Where I used to live."

"That must be a blast," mused Rip, "living in L.A. and going surfing every day. Did you ever surf, Cupidity?"

"No, mostly I played pool and smoked cigars," she answered with a glance at Laura.

"That's my girl!" exclaimed Cody with

a laugh. He gripped her tightly around the waist, making it difficult for them to walk very quickly across the pitted parking lot. Rip held Laura's hand, which was welcome, because her hands were freezing.

They circled around to the rear of the building, where a couple of skaters were standing in the shadows. The grimy warehouse had to be three stories high, and a row of windows across the top were all broken. The muffled music seemed to be coming from deep underground, and a strange smell wafted from the aged railroad tracks in the rear. They walked toward a pair of metal doors that were set at a sloping angle in the brick wall. Farther away a door opened, and a gang of giggling girls staggered out on their high heels.

The doormen approached the foursome, shining a flashlight in their faces. "Cody! Rip!" they shouted when they recognized the guys. They exchanged skaters' handshakes and punched each other in the shoulders like old friends.

"Dudes, you have picked a primo night to party with us!" said the bigger of the two guards. "We're grindin' it tonight."

"Cool," said Rip. "You got a band or a sound system?"

"Sound system," answered the other doorman. "Like normally we would have to charge you five bucks each, but hot chicks like these two are always free." They couldn't take their eyes off Cupidity.

The new girl winked at Laura and said, "It's good to be hot."

Laura shivered, and her teeth chattered. "I don't feel hot at the moment."

"Here's your ten," said Cody, taking a crumpled bill from his pocket and paying for Rip, too. "The party's on me."

Cupidity gave him a grateful smile. "Thanks, sweetie, but we're not going to get busted here, are we?"

"Can't promise that, but you are going to skate to get in," said the smaller doorman. His partner pulled open the metal doors and revealed a long chute that led down into darkness and the din of a party. With a gulp, Laura realized that it was an old coal chute descending to the furnace room, probably long abandoned.

She laughed nervously. "I can't slide down there, I'll get all dirty. I'll take the door."

"You're not sliding." The big doorman pointed to what looked like a pile of lumber, but it was really a pile of old skateboards. Laura saw one of the girls teeter over to the pile and add a board to it. "Everybody skates down, especially first-timers," he explained. "It doesn't matter how hot you are."

Rip put a comforting hand on her shoulder. "There's like air mattresses and pillows down there. I'll go first and look out for you, and you just go down on your knees."

"On my knees?" she asked doubtfully, glad she had worn jeans.

"Come on!" called Cupidity, grabbing a battered old skateboard and heading for the door. Without a moment's hesitation, she knelt on the skateboard and pushed herself down the old metal chute, which rattled under the small wheels. Her delighted squeals pierced the night.

Cody took a board and hurtled down the chute in a crouch, and Rip was right behind him. He gave Laura an encouraging smile and a wave before he plunged into the darkness. Shivering more than ever, she grabbed a skateboard and noted the smirks on the doormen's faces.

"If I have to go to the hospital," she said, "I want to go to Mid City General."

"That's our favorite," answered the shorter one.

With a gulp, Laura edged toward the door and the dark chute. Once she got close, she realized that there was light and gaiety at the other end, along with many mattresses, which Rip was busy arranging for her. It was probably only twenty feet and not as steep as she feared; there was no sense putting it off.

"Xena!" she shouted as she had when she was a little girl, flinging her knees onto the skateboard and shooting into space.

Immediately she knew she was in trouble, as the wheels ground and squealed on the old sheet of metal. Certain she was going to fall off, Laura gripped the front of the board with her hands and screamed. The wild ride reminded her of sledding, which also scared her. Before she could catch her breath, she flew into space and landed in a comforting cloud of old mattresses, followed by Rip's strong arms.

For no good reason, he needed to fall onto the mattress with her and grab her shivering torso. Rip nuzzled her and gave her a brief kiss, which warmed her up at once. "You all right?" he asked with concern.

I'm good enough to kiss, she thought happily. Instead she smiled and said, "Can I get up and make sure I'm in one piece?"

"Oh, you're in one piece," he said, giving her body an extra squeeze. "What are you drinking?"

"Something legal," she answered.

Rip slid off her and vanished into the crowd, which was barely lit by a few strobes and some hokey discotheque lights. Pools of light and people were scattered throughout the huge basement, especially around the disc jockey and his sound system, but there didn't seem to be any good reason to light this dingy space. With all the smoke, it would be hard to see anyway.

Against the wall was a stairwell, which led to the exit they had seen before, and it was well marked by a sign. Some brawny straight-faced guys looked as if they were on security, but the crowd wasn't fighting.

It wasn't as warm as Laura had hoped, but the crush of bodies and promise of dancing gave her some hope.

Cupidity bumped into her and shouted over the music, "Hey, princess, what do you think?"

Laura looked around at the funky surroundings and loud revelers and answered, "I just realized, skaters wear more corporate logos than anybody."

"No, I meant the *boys*!" said Cupidity, looking a bit frustrated. "Do you like Cody?"

Laura narrowed her eyes suspiciously at the new girl. "Why are you always trying to give me your dates? I have one of my own, and he can't keep his hands off me."

"Good," said Cupidity with a sigh. "So you like him and things are clicking. I was . . . I was asking about Cody for me, of course. I think he should ask me to Homecoming, even though I can't go."

"Why can't you go?"

"Well, I've got to go out of town that weekend," she answered. "Some family business in L.A.—it can't be changed. I may have to leave suddenly, so if you see that I'm gone, don't worry about it."

Laura tried not to look concerned about this information, because Cupidity was Cupidity. Still it got her thinking about her mission to compare her friend's fancy bow with the one Cupid had in Pompeii. Maybe she was all wrong about the girl's matchmaking skills, but she had to put her mind at ease.

"Homecoming is still a long shot," complained Laura. "Skater dudes aren't known for going to Homecoming."

Cupidity flipped her golden tresses and laughed. "Don't worry about that—these skater dudes will go to Homecoming and be happy about it."

Muscling through the rowdy crowd came Cody and Rip, carrying cans of some high-caffeine, high-energy drink. Rip also balanced a bowl full of potato chips on his head. The girls relieved them of their burdens, and they stepped away from the coal chute as more partygoers dropped in.

"Hey, I found a place to sit down!" announced Cody, yelling over the din.

"Where?" asked Laura doubtfully. She didn't see any furniture, not even a folding chair.

"On those mattresses on the floor, against the wall," replied Cody. "Come on!"

Carrying all their supplies, they trekked across the run-down warehouse basement until they reached a very shadowy, bad-smelling corner, where partyers lay sprawled about in odd positions. *This is the make-out place,* Laura realized, *and maybe the restroom, too.*

She pushed her drink back into Rip's hands and said, "I like this song! Don't you want to dance?"

Numbly he nodded his head, and Laura grabbed Cupidity's hand and pulled her back toward the masses. "Come on, we've got to shake some booty!"

"Yeah, thanks!" replied Cupidity as if she was glad to be rescued. Once they got to the dance floor, the new girl shed her coat and began to shake everything she had, which was a lot. To a frenzied song by some angry band, Cupidity gyrated wildly until she had every boy in the warehouse drooling over her. The girls glared at the stunning show-off, except for a few who were stomping along with the boys.

Cody was entranced by Cupidity's performance, and Rip watched his friend's date while he tried to talk to a third girl. Nobody was watching Laura, and she realized that this would be a good time to slip out to the car to inspect Cupidity's bow. She danced her way against the flow of the crowd until she made it to the stairway. Then Laura ran upward without even looking back.

The cool night air smelled wonderful after the smoke and odd odors below. The two skater doormen gave her a look as she walked past, but they were occupied with new arrivals. Laura dashed over the muddy, uneven parking lot until she reached Cupidity's yellow convertible, which stood out like a lighthouse. Earlier in the evening, she had seen Cupidity pull a lever under the dashboard to open the trunk of her car, which was a trusting way to secure it when she left the top down. But Cupidity didn't seem to be bothered by the things that bothered other people.

It took a bit of searching, but Laura managed to find all the levers—for the gas, the front hood, and the trunk. She stole a glance around to make sure nobody was watching her, and she saw nothing but silent cars in the unlit parking lot. With a rush of adrenaline, Laura popped the trunk and scrambled to the back of the sports car to see what she could find.

The courtesy light in the trunk came on, and there was her purse, right beside Cupidity's duffel bag. Laura reached for the bag to make sure it contained the precious bow and arrows, and she could feel the slender, carved lines of the aged weapon. It had to be specially made for someone so short. With trembling hands, she unzipped the bag and reached inside to pull out the bow. Laura had held the bag itself before, but she had touched the bow only once, briefly, on the first day when Cupidity had pulled it out of her locker.

She was going to use it even then, thought Laura with a shudder. *I should have seen it at the time, but who expects the supernatural in Denton, Ohio?*

Even as she drew the bow out of the duffel bag, she knew it was not just a curved piece of wood with the string already taut, ready for immediate use. No, this was an ancient artifact that had been painted many times, including very recently. It was now light brown, trying to look like a normal child's bow, but she could easily tell that it had once been gilded in gold, painted in gleaming white enamel, and encrusted with jewels. She didn't even need to take the photocopied picture out of her pocket to tell.

This is Cupid's bow, only Cupid is a girl. When did that happen?

An owl hooted somewhere overhead, probably from the broken windows of the deserted warehouse's top floor. Taking a deep breath, Laura reached back into the bag for the next piece of the puzzle. As soon as her fingers touched an arrow, it seemed to spring into her grasp as if eager to be unleashed.

She slowly lifted the old-fashioned missile from the bag and marveled at its intricate design and workmanship. The arrow tip was gleaming and sharp, but it seemed to be made of moonbeams that passed right through her fingers. The feathers of the fletching were as long and delicate as an eyelash, yet as stiff as a knife blade; they bristled from the shaft in vibrant colors, like the light beams from a prism.

Her hands trembled, yet her recent archery lesson came back to her as she lifted the bow and nocked the arrow to the string. The night wind sent a primitive feeling of power coursing through her veins, as if she were the greatest hunter in the world. Laura could imagine herself on the prowl, stalking the elusive prey—man and woman. Involuntarily, she drew back the arrow, and the bowstring tightened. Her arms tingled as if a current had suddenly connected through them, and her muscles ached to unleash the magical missile.

"No!" shouted a voice. Laura was startled and whirled in the direction of the sound just as she lost her grip on the shaft. The arrow flew straight from her hands and into Cupidity's heaving chest.

"Urrgh!" exclaimed Cupidity with a groan, and she staggered backward from the impact.

"They're not real arrows!" cried Laura, who was suddenly hysterical with the fear that she might have hurt Cupidity. "The points aren't real!" She reached into the duffel bag to pull out another arrow, and she pointed it toward Cupidity, who was still staggering about.

"What are you doing? You psycho!" yelled a male voice. Cody charged between them, as angry as a young bull. All he could see was Cupidity flailing her arms helplessly, while her crazy friend pointed a bow and arrow at her.

"Give me that!" ordered Cody, lunging for the weapon. Laura flinched and poked him in the wrist with the arrow tip, and the arrow disappeared. "Ow!" he cried, recoiling as if from a shock.

While Cupidity crawled on the ground in the dirty parking lot, Cody began to twitch and gurgle. Laura gasped and watched in horror as his face went through a multitude of changes—disbelief, a flare of anger, followed by a puzzled expression as if he had forgotten where he was. A moment later, the dark lord of the skaters looked as if he would burst into tears.

"Cupidity!" he wailed.

Nine

Laura felt as if *she* was the one who'd been shot with an arrow in that dingy parking lot outside the skaters' rave. She didn't really start breathing again until she was sure that Cupidity and Cody were not seriously hurt by her careless missiles. Then she remembered that physical injury wasn't the real danger from Cupidity's arrows.

When Cody spotted Cupidity, he rushed to her side and gently picked her up from the ground, all the while kissing her like a puppy who was glad to see his master. "Are you all right? Are you hurt?" he asked worriedly. "Oh, no, you skinned your knee!"

"It's nothing," she rasped, holding onto his arm for support. When she looked into his eyes, Cupidity broke into a dazed but ecstatic smile. "I couldn't be better . . . no way."

Laura nervously approached them, wringing her hands. "Uh, Cupidity," she asked, "do you know what happened to you?"

"What happened to me?" she repeated, looking as if her brain had been fried. All Cupidity could manage to do was hang on to Cody's arm, although both of them were swaying uncertainly on their feet. "I found my skater punk dude," she muttered, "that's what happened to me."

"Uh, yeah, for sure," agreed Cody. His trademark sneer completely gone, he gazed fondly at the petite blond. "I found my very own goddess tonight, and I'll never leave her side."

"Oh, no." Laura groaned and covered her eyes.

"Codykins," asked Cupidity, batting her eyelashes at him, "will you go with me to the Homecoming Dance?"

"Whatever you want, Cupie Doll." They hugged each other blissfully.

"This is too much," murmured Laura, starting to panic. The ornate bow was still in her hand, and she waved it like a life preserver. "Cupidity, look at this bow! Don't you remember what you used to do with it?"

"Archery practice," answered the girl with a nod, then she snuggled into Cody's armpit. "I'm giving up archery."

"Don't you know what your name means?" asked Laura, begging her to come to her senses. Although she had never admitted to being Cupid, the new girl didn't seem to be putting on an act. She had been honestly smitten with her own dumb love bolt, just like Emma and Jake . . . Megan and Peter . . . and how many others!

"How do you reverse the spell?" Laura pleaded.

Cupidity just giggled and hugged Cody. "You're crazy, girl. I don't care that you got into my trunk and messed with my bow, I just didn't want you to hurt anyone. You don't need to come up with a wacky story to explain it."

"You're *Cupid*!" shrieked Laura. "Don't you know who Cupid is?"

"Sure, we know who Cupid is," answered Cody, "one of Santa's reindeers."

"That's so true!" chirped Cupidity, hugging him tighter. "You're so smart, Codykins! Let's go back inside and find one of those mattresses."

"Good idea," answered the skater dude, looking as if he had been brainwashed.

Laura wanted to scream, but instead she tried a desperate ruse. "I've got a terrible headache—can we end the date early and go home?"

"No," they answered in unison, turning their backs on her. Looking like the most darling, devoted couple, Cupidity and Cody ambled arm in arm back to the party.

"Oh, you idiot!" Laura yelled at herself. "What have you done?" She threw the magic bow back into the trunk as if it were a live snake, then grabbed her purse and slammed the trunk shut.

Maybe Cupidity is just pretending to have amnesia, Laura told herself. *Maybe she's only punking me in order to stick to her lame cover story. But I shot her with one of her own arrows and pricked Cody a moment later—it's got to have had some effect! The two of them are exactly like the other Stepford Lovebirds.*

Laura stomped around the darkened parking lot, trying to forget the distant laughter and music, because she had to think. There were two possible explanations. One was that the Roman god Cupid was real, that she was living as a teenage girl in Denton, Ohio, and that she had just gotten amnesia. The other possibility was that Laura Sweeney was insane. At this point, she wasn't sure which explanation she preferred.

I might need proof, she told herself. Laura looked around to make sure that Cupidity and Cody had gone and left her by herself in the parking lot. That alone was suspicious behavior, because normally Cupidity wouldn't leave her bow and arrows for Laura to use again. She had rushed out here to stop Laura from handling the bow, and now she was willing to just walk away from it. That didn't seem likely.

For the second time that night Laura reached under the dashboard and pulled the lever to open the trunk. Gingerly she grabbed the bow and put it back into the duffel bag, making sure not to touch any of the arrows. After shooting the bow, Laura was sure it had powerful magic—so powerful that Cupid didn't have to be the one using it.

I could have the power of Cupid, she realized. *But I don't want it, especially if I might make as many bad decisions as Cupidity has. Look at the ridiculous couple I just created!* she thought in despair. *No, this is too much power for any teenager to have. But then again, what if I need proof?*

Despite her misgivings Laura again grabbed the duffel bag, stealing Cupidity's bow and arrows. She looked around and slammed the trunk lid shut before scurrying into the darkness.

As she walked back to the road, Laura pulled her cell phone out of her purse and dialed a taxicab company. Normally she would have called a friend, like Taryn, but Taryn was out with Chester tonight. Plus she didn't want to have to explain carrying a large duffel bag on a blind date, or what had happened on that blind date. Love was still in the air, like the flu, and Laura felt bad about making the epidemic worse.

Laura gave the taxi company her general location, then checked to make sure she had enough money to get home. *I'll figure it out,* she told herself. *I'll do something to correct this.*

In time, headlights cruised down the road, coming toward her, and she recognized the slow-moving vehicle as her taxi. Laura waved it down and bounded into the back seat, anxious to get out of there. As she clutched the precious duffel bag to her chest, she realized that magical weapons could turn their bearers evil or insane. She knew she was taking a terrible chance keeping the bow and arrows, but it was a great relief to know the truth, especially about Peter Yarmench.

It's not Peter's fault that he's in love with Megan—he's under a spell, in the clutches of her undeserved affection. I have to save him!

Laura worried all night about what had happened and what to do, and by morning she was bleary-eyed and confused. She had almost convinced herself that she had to be crazy—no bow and arrow could make normal people fall madly in love with people they hated. Although it seemed that was exactly what had happened, especially with Jake and Emma. But then again, hate and love were similar, she had always been told, and maybe she had just let Peter be stolen by Megan. Only one person could really solve this mystery and tell her the truth: Cupidity.

So by eight o'clock Saturday morning Laura was waiting at the door of Cupidity's apartment, stomping her foot. She had already rung the doorbell twice, and then she heard stumbling sounds from inside. Laura was about to ring the doorbell a third time when it finally creaked open; looking disheveled and sleepy, Cupidity peered out through the slit.

"Laura," she croaked. "What are you doing here? There isn't school on Saturday, is there?"

"No." Laura pushed her glasses up her nose and tried to stay calm. "Can I come in and talk to you for a moment?" When the other girl seemed hesitant, Laura added, "It's an emergency."

"Oh, emergency," muttered Cupidity as she opened the door. "Hey, what happened to you last night? You disappeared on us!"

"Remember me telling you I didn't feel well?" answered Laura. "Well, I went home early. Besides, you didn't need me."

Cupidity smiled wistfully and scratched her ribs through her silky nightgown. "No, we sure didn't need you. What a dreamy night."

"You and Cody—" Laura wiggled her fingers instead of saying more.

"Me and Cody did what?" asked Cupidity, sounding offended. "He was a perfect gentleman—more or less . . ." She strode into her living room and began to pick up various bits of trash. When she found the cigars on the mantel, she wrinkled her nose and touched them as if they were bugs.

"Ew! Where did these come from?" The blond girl marched into the kitchen and threw the cigars into the trash.

"Wait a second," said Laura. "You were smoking those cigars last time I was here."

"As if!" shrieked Cupidity, sounding totally offended. "My dad must have left them here. What's going on with you, Laura? You didn't make any sense last night either."

Laura stared intently at her friend and begged, "Please remember what happened last night. You're forgetting something important. You left the rave, came outside to your car, and found me holding your bow. You shouted at me to stop—do you remember that?"

"Yeah," she answered doubtfully. "Sure, I remember it. But mostly I remember Cody." A blissful look swept across her innocent face.

"I know we can't forget Cody," said Laura, trying not to get frustrated, "but that wasn't on your mind when you shouted at me. You didn't want me to hold your bow . . . because . . . because?"

"Because I didn't want you to hurt Cody." Cupidity smiled sweetly at the thought of her beloved. "He's so smart and cute."

Laura rubbed her face, knocking her glasses askew. "All right. Let's back up a bit. Where did you say you grew up?"

Cupidity scowled. "What are you, my guidance counselor? I get asked questions all week long in school, and now I have to answer questions on Saturday?"

"You don't know where you grew up,"

declared Laura, "because you have amnesia. Last night you lost your memory."

"That's ridiculous," scoffed Cupidity. "I know *you*—I know my friends . . . and my boyfriend. And I know how you ditched poor Rip last night. Poor boy was heartbroken. Those skaters are like really sensitive, you know."

Laura sputtered with disbelief. "You've known all of us for a whole week! Do you remember your old friends, before you moved here?"

"I told you . . . I was homeschooled!" Cupidity folded her arms and stomped into the living room. "I don't care about my past, anyway. My life begins *now* . . . now that I've found Cody."

Laura followed her friend across the room, waving her arms. "But you've got to care, because that proves that you've lost your memory. The bow and arrows—don't you know what they *do*?"

"I don't care about the stupid bow," replied Cupidity. "You can keep it—you're the one obsessed with it!" When the phone rang, she dashed toward the device as if she already knew who it was.

"Hello, Codykins!" she cooed, slumping into an overstuffed chair. "Yes, I've been longing to hear your voice! Laura is over here now, and she's being a real grump. She doesn't even *care* that she devastated poor Rip last night. And she keeps asking me all kinds of weird questions about my past. Do you care about my past?"

She giggled and curled into a cute ball. "I didn't think so." After a moment, Cupidity looked up at her guest and said, "This is private stuff, Laura. Good-bye. And don't bring the bow and arrows to school anymore, like you did before. You'll get us in trouble."

While Laura clenched her fists and her mouth, Cupidity went right on babbling to her boyfriend. After a moment, her conversation degenerated into gooey baby talk, and Laura had to flee from the apartment. She climbed back into her mom's car and pounded her fists on the steering wheel.

I can't help any of them, she despaired. *They're doomed to mindless, pointless love.* From her misery, Laura thought of another friend who might be more helpful than Cupidity had been. She scrounged around in her purse for her cell phone and dialed Taryn's number.

"Good morning!" said an incredibly bright, cheerful voice.

"Taryn?" asked Laura uncertainly. "Is that you?"

"Well, of course it's me," she chirped. "I had a great time on my date last night. First of all, I wore my new tank top, the blue one—"

"Listen, I'd really love to hear this," lied Laura, "but I'm driving and I've only got a moment. Can I get a phone number from you and then call you back?"

"Hey, how was your date last night?" asked Taryn, oblivious to everything but love. "Did you hook up?"

"Yeah, he kissed me," said Laura, glad she could tell the truth. "Listen, what's the name of that psychic you once told me about? The Conjure Woman, you called her."

"Oooh," breathed Taryn, sounding impressed. "The one with the love spells? Are you that serious about someone? I want to warn you, Laura, once you get involved in that stuff, you may not be able to get out. It can backfire on you, too."

"No kidding," said Laura sharply. "The number, please?"

"I'm looking! Madame Luisa is her name, or something like that." Taryn breathed a triumphant sigh. "Ah, here's the number."

As she rattled it off, Laura wrote it down on a slip of paper. She was uncertain whether she would have the courage to call the Conjure Woman, but she had to get help from somewhere. "Thanks," she answered glumly.

"Are you sure about this?" asked Taryn, "I didn't figure you to believe in love spells and stuff."

"Well, some things have changed my mind lately," admitted Laura. "What are you doing tonight?"

"Going out with Chester again," answered Taryn in a dreamy tone of voice. "And you?"

Laura shook her head. "I'm not sure yet, but I'll call you back later. I *do* want to hear about your date, really."

"Yeah," answered Taryn, "and since you're

hunting for love potions, I want to hear about your date too."

Laura said good-bye and clicked off her cell phone. She stared at the number in her lap, wondering if she had the courage to call it. But doing nothing meant leaving things exactly the way they were, and that was unacceptable.

With determination Laura dialed the number. Nervously she tapped her steering wheel as the phone rang. Finally a sleepy voice answered, "Hello."

"Hello, I'm looking for Madame Luisa," she began.

"Well, you found her . . . at an ungodly time of the morning, I might add. What can I do for you?"

Laura gulped. "I need to see you."

"I can give you an appointment next Wednesday—"

"No!" exclaimed Laura. "I need to see you today!"

She heard a low grumble. "I'm booked up all day, from ten o'clock on."

"It's not even nine o'clock yet," said Laura. "Please! I'm desperate."

"Aren't they all?" muttered the sleepy

Conjure Woman. "Do you have my address?"

"No, but I'm ready to write it down."

"Bring forty bucks with you too," added Madame Luisa.

Laura didn't know what to expect from the Conjure Woman's home, but she was still a little surprised to find a typical split-level ranch house in a nice part of town. Of course there weren't any steamy swamps in Denton, Ohio, so it might be hard to find a shack surrounded by gators and lightning bugs. Running around in the front yard were three little kids, wearing bath towels as if they were capes, and Laura had to dodge them on her way to the front door.

The door opened before she reached it, and Laura found herself confronted by a very tall woman with dusky skin but bright blond hair. She was dressed in jeans, a T-shirt, and a long cardigan sweater with a chain around her waist.

Madame Luisa looked surprised at the sight of her visitor. "You're a teenager? What problem can you have, being young and cute?"

"Plenty," answered Laura. "May I come in?"

"Sure, my consulting room is in the back. I've got a pot of tea brewing." Leading the way, the statuesque woman led her customer through a neat living room, down a long hallway, and into a bedroom in the back of the house. Looking around, Laura felt better, because this room was very atmospheric, with walls bedecked in religious symbols, candles, and artwork from around the world.

"You have all the bases covered," said Laura in amazement. She didn't add that Cupidity's bow would fit right in with the clutter of artifacts on the walls.

Madame Luisa shrugged. "You never know. Normally in a case like yours, I recommend Blue Succory. It makes a wonderful love potion—you can blow the powder up his nose or put it in his underwear, next to his skin."

Laura sat solemnly at the table and chose her words carefully. "That's not my problem. I'm looking for an anti-love potion."

The Conjure Woman sat at the table, scratching her blond hair. She gazed curiously at the girl and asked, "You want to get rid of a guy, right? I've got something you can put in your bath water—make you smell like a week-old fish."

"Ah, it's not something for me," said Laura carefully. "I can make people fall in love with each other, I just can't make them fall out of love."

"Is that right?" growled the tall woman, sitting back in her chair and looking very skeptical. "If you could really do that, then you'd ride up here in a limousine."

Laura leaned forward and narrowed her eyes at the Conjure Woman, hoping to convince her how serious she was. "If I can prove it to you, will you help me?"

Madame Luisa scowled. "How are you going to do that?"

Laura took a deep breath, then blurted, "You must have couples that you're supposed to get together. So give me one—their names, addresses, and stuff—and I'll make sure they hook up. I'll do your job for you, but just this once and with a pair who really deserve to be together."

"Whoa," replied Madame Luisa, looking impressed. "You seem to have confidence in this skill of yours. Okay, I'm going to give you a file, and you're going to fix them up."

She rose from her chair and walked to a closet, took a key from the chain around her waist, and unlocked the door. Madame Luisa disappeared inside the closet, but her voice boomed, "Honey, it's not fair that you know all about me—where I live, what my kids look like—and I don't know nothin' about you. Giving you this file, I'm putting a lot of faith in you . . ."

"I'll give you my address and phone number," offered Laura.

"There's pen and paper by the teapot."

Laura dutifully wrote down her details, wondering whether Madame Luisa was for real. She didn't want to put powder into people's underwear, and she really doubted if that would help. But she had made the offer, and she had wisely kept quiet about Cupidity's bow.

The Conjure Woman stepped out of the closet holding a file folder, and she carefully locked the door behind her. "Okay, your assignment is to put these two oldsters together," she said, tossing the folder onto the table. "She's rich, and she's my client. They're truly in love, but he won't marry her because he's proud about money and his independence. Otherwise, they'd be hitched. So you really only have to work on him."

"They'll both be completely smitten by tomorrow," Laura promised grimly. She opened the folder to find photos and extensive notes about one of the wealthiest and most famous women in town, Dorothy Planchett. "Wow, she has trouble finding a husband?"

"No, she's got him going, but he just has issues," said Madame Luisa. "You think you can wipe them out?"

Laura closed the folder and rose to her feet. "Mr. Barclay won't know what hit him. I'm going to do you this favor to prove that what I say is true. But in return you need to promise me that you will show me how to make people fall *out* of love."

The Conjure Woman picked up the paper with Laura's information. "Hey, I'm good for it. I didn't charge you the usual forty bucks, did I, Laura Sweeney?"

"No," she answered, moving toward the door, "but I need more than a discount—I need help."

Madame Luisa didn't say anything as she escorted Laura Sweeney outside to her car, and the cautious girl locked the file folder in her trunk. The Conjure Woman didn't entirely believe her story, but she knew when people were sincere—and desperate. The girl believed she could conjure love spells, even if she couldn't.

As soon as Laura drove away, Luisa pulled a cell phone out of her sweater pocket and dialed a number. "Arnie, it's me. Get your notebook, because I've got a job for you. I want you to tail somebody for me."

Ten

Laura felt like a stalker. Not only that, but she was armed with what looked like a deadly weapon. Thinking about how shady she must look, she crouched in the hedges running along the parking lot of the Institute for the Blind in downtown Denton. She had checked the social calendar in the newspaper and found that Mrs. Dorothy Planchett was attending a fundraiser for the institute that night, and Mr. Roger Barclay was also scheduled to attend.

It was nearly ten o'clock at night, and the event had started at six. Well-dressed people were beginning to leave, and her chance was coming—but so was an attack of the nerves. Shooting Cupidity and Cody in the parking lot had been an accident, but deliberately turning this powerful love spell on two strangers was difficult. It didn't really help to know that one of them had asked for it.

What if I miss? thought Laura. *I'm not half the archer Cupidity is.* She thought about waiting for the couple at Dorothy Planchett's mansion, but the place was a fortress with a high brick wall. Plus she had no guarantee that they would be going back there after the fund-raiser. It was here and now—this might be her only chance. At least the bow was a silent weapon.

The night was dark with no moon, but the parking lot was brightly lit and Laura could see clearly. But then again, so could everyone else. What if she was caught? Not everyone coming out of the institute was blind. And in fact, the lovebirds might be with other people.

Wait a minute, she told herself, *I don't actually have to shoot them with the arrows. I only had to poke Cody with one by accident, and that worked.* She had a feeling that the second arrow would find its mark without much trouble, because love gathered momentum once it was launched.

Laura was distracted by a burst of laughter, and she turned to see six elegantly dressed attendees emerge from the institute. Catching her breath, she lifted her binoculars and watched them amble down the walkway to the parking lot, talking and laughing. She instantly recognized her quarry, that distinguished older couple Dorothy Planchett and Roger Barclay. How was she going to do this? The parking lot was starting to get crowded with people.

If I'm not careful, I'm gonna end up in jail, Laura thought ruefully. She realized that every time Cupidity shot her little bow, there had always been a distraction. The paintball attack, the fight between Jake and Peter—that's why she didn't get caught. Laura worked her way through the bushes, braving the thorns and stickers until she reached the other side. Then she screamed as loudly as she could.

That stopped the partygoers in their tracks, and they shouted and pointed. To make sure, Laura grabbed the bushes and shook them as she screamed again. Dorothy and Roger hurried over to check it out, while Laura dashed around the end of the hedgerow in order to flank them. While they were searching the bushes, she hoped to catch them from behind.

Laura was reaching into the duffel bag to grab the bow and arrow when she ran right into a chubby security guard. "What is going on?" he asked her nervously. "I heard a scream!"

"Robbers!" she answered, clutching the duffel bag to her chest. "They tried to steal my purse, then they hauled somebody else into the bushes. There they are!" Laura pointed to the two dark figures forty feet away, crawling among the hedges.

Looking jittery, the security officer drew his club. "I'll fix them. You wait here!"

She didn't wait there but followed the guard at a discreet distance. She saw him grab the distinguished older man and threaten him with his club, while Dorothy Planchett began to argue and point at the bushes.

There was no more time to think about it. Laura grabbed her bow and arrow and let the duffel bag fall to the ground. While everyone was busy talking at once, she nocked the arrow to the string, pulled it back, took careful aim at Mrs. Planchett, and let fly. The arrow streaked through the darkness into the clutch of people, and she heard a loud yelp.

Before she had any more time to think about it, Laura grabbed another arrow and nocked it to the bow. Now people were looking around, trying to figure out what was happening. The security guard walked back toward her, waving his hands, and she cut loose with the second arrow. It was intended for Roger Barclay, but the brave security guard jumped in front of the arrow and took it in the chest.

"Oops," said Laura, quickly jumping into the bushes and ducking out of sight.

She didn't have to worry about the security guard anymore, because he staggered for a few steps, then keeled over onto his stomach. Dorothy Planchett ran to comfort the fallen guard, and she slumped over him and cried, the same way Megan had wailed over Peter. Roger Barclay just stood around, looking confused.

There was great commotion, someone went to call an ambulance, and the parking lot was soon full of concerned people. In due time, it became clear that nobody was really hurt, but Dorothy Planchett was distraught over the security guard. While the rich widow fussed and fawned over the dazed man, Laura tried to sneak away.

"Thanks," said a voice in the darkness. "You just made my richest client fall in love with a nobody half her age."

Laura skidded to a stop as Madame Luisa stepped out of the shadows, staring grimly at her. There was a seedy man lurking behind her, wearing a dark suit and a Panama hat.

"Madame Luisa!" said Laura with a start. "What are you doing here?"

"Came to see how you work your miracles," answered the Conjure Woman, stepping toward her. "You're not impressive, but that little archery set sure is."

Laura clutched the duffel bag protectively. "I . . . I don't know what you're talking about."

"I'm a big strong woman, and you're just a little slip of a girl," said Madame

Luisa with a sly smile. "What's to keep me from just *taking* it from you?"

"Nothing," replied Laura evenly. "But I warn you . . . this bow is cursed. Your own love life will nose-dive, and you may totally freak out—like the person I stole it from. She doesn't even know who she is."

The imposing woman narrowed her eyes and gazed deeply into Laura's soul. The girl felt herself tremble as the Conjure Woman studied her, but she had been honest, and so she was able to stand her ground.

"Bless me, child, you're telling the truth," said Luisa, her voice barely a whisper. "You're right, it is bad juju to steal an item of power. I just wouldn't feel right about doing that."

Laura breathed a sigh of relief. "Oh, good. Then you'll help me reverse the spell?"

"I wouldn't feel right about it," said Madame Luisa, "but my friend Arnie doesn't care so much." She snapped her fingers, and her henchman rushed forward and tried to grab the duffel bag out of Laura's hands.

Laura struggled and managed to hang on, even though she was tossed around the parking lot like an old rag. Finally she let out the same piercing scream she had used earlier, only now it really was a plea for help. "Robbers! Robbers!" she shouted.

Her cries attracted attention, and three onlookers started walking toward them. "Arnie, let's get out of here!" hissed Madame Luisa. "She'll let her guard down eventually." With a malevolent glare at Laura, the Conjure Woman slipped away into the darkness, followed by her hired thug.

"This magic stuff really sucks," muttered Laura as she shoved the duffel bag into the bushes. When the partygoers reached her, she pointed after the fleeing figures. "They took my purse. Please get it back!"

"Absolutely," said one of the men, charging after the fleeing pair. Another followed him, and the third man looked at Laura with concern.

"Are you all right?" he asked. "What the heck is going on here?"

"Purse thieves," she answered breathlessly. "They hit us all at once. Better get after them!"

"Okay." The man nodded and took off,

and Laura dragged the duffel bag out of the bushes and dashed in the other direction. She was so scared and upset that she didn't stop running until she was almost home.

Oh, what am I going to do? thought Laura desperately. *Peter is in love with that stuck-up Megan. Cupidity is so ga-ga over Cody that she's forgotten who she is. Jake the jock is madly in love with über-Goth Emma, which has thrown the entire social order of the school out of whack. The Conjure Woman is trying to steal the bow from me. I just made the wrong couple fall crazy in love, and I still don't have a date for the Homecoming Dance!*

Only one thing was certain, Laura decided grimly: Cupidity's bow and arrows were the real deal.

Monday at school was awful, because it seemed as if everybody was part of a blissfully happy twosome except for Laura. Plus all day long she imagined that Madame Luisa and her evil henchman were stalking her, trying to find the magic bow. It wasn't there—it was in Laura's locker with a brandnew combination lock, but that wasn't very comforting. Not only did she have a weapon at school, but any moron could break into a locker. It happened every day.

Also, it seemed that the entire school was in the throes of preparation for Homecoming, only two weeks away. Fimbrey was a basketball school, and the football team was often mediocre. Still it was a big deal when they came home to play after their road trips to Marion and Mansfield, and the Homecoming Dance was as big as the spring formal. Watching all of her friends, from Taryn to Cupidity, making big plans for the dance made Laura even more depressed.

But it was Cupidity who delivered the final blow. With Cody lurking only a few feet behind her, she ambushed Laura in the hallway after lunch. "Sweeney, I have to talk to you," said Cupidity importantly.

Laura stopped and forced a smile as she turned around. "Yes?"

The petite blond crossed her arms and looked quite stern. "Cody and I agree—we don't want you around anymore in the Cupidity group."

"Because you're a nut!" added Cody from the cheap seats.

Laura's mouth hung open. "The Cupidity group? Sounds like an online dating company. Are you saying you don't want to be friends with me anymore?"

"That's right," answered Cupidity, "and you've got to stay away from my other friends, like Jake, Megan, and Peter."

"What?" asked Laura, aghast. "That's ridiculous! I haven't done anything to any of you."

Well, except for accidentally hook you up with Cody, Laura thought. *But she's deliberately pulled the same trick on lots of people, only she doesn't remember.*

"There's just something weird about you," said Cupidity. "The way you like that bow and arrows . . . and all those old Roman gods."

"*Me?*" responded Laura in amazement. "You say *I'm* weird, when you can't even remember what you were doing a week ago? And the bow and arrows belong to *you*!"

"Yeah," said Cupidity with a puzzled expression, "I can't remember why I bought those things. But anyway, you need to be more normal again before you can hang with us."

Laura rolled her eyes. "Whatever. If you only knew how abnormal *you* are."

"Hey, who are you calling abnormal?" snapped Cody, swaggering up to Laura. "That's my woman you're talking about . . . and the future Homecoming Queen. Maybe the future Mrs. Cody Kenyon."

Laura tried not to cringe. After all, it wasn't entirely his fault he was goofy in love. "I hope you'll be very happy," she said, although she was plotting how to break them up. "But you can't tell me who to be friends with."

"We'll see about that," said Cupidity with a sniff. She whirled on her heel and marched away, while Cody gave Laura his trademark sneer.

Laura went through the rest of the day in a blur. She felt that the whole school was looking at her, pointing her out as the girl who was condemned by Cupidity. Taryn and her old buds were friendly to her, but they only wanted to talk about boys, the dance, and boys. Laura was fed up with romance; it seemed like a fever that had affected all their minds.

The funk lasted all day until she caught

sight of Peter Yarmench, waiting for her after her last class. Laura looked around to make sure that Megan and Cupidity weren't going to ambush her, but they didn't seem to be around. The hallway was crowded, and Peter was standing in an alcove by the drinking fountain.

Laura tried to act cheerful as she approached him. "Hi!"

"Hi," he answered, looking down as if he were embarrassed. "I heard about what Cupidity said to you, and I think she's really out of line."

"Thanks," answered Laura, smiling for real.

"So what if you're a little whacko," said Peter. "We all get that way sometimes."

Laura frowned. "How am I whacko?"

"Well, you stole Cupidity's bow and arrows and made her out to be a nutcase," answered Peter. "And you ditched three people in the middle of a double date."

"I remember that you once ditched *me* on a double date," said Laura, glowering at him. "There's a lot more to this than you understand, Peter."

He leaned against the wall and smiled.

"And Taryn told me that you went to see some kind of witch doctor . . . the Conjure Woman?"

"That loudmouth," muttered Laura. "Forget about my problems. Look around you, Peter. Look at yourself. You've never dated anyone in this school before, and now you're dating the head cheerleader. The Prince of the Preppies is going out with the Queen of the Goths. Homeboys are dating geeks, skaters are with debutantes—it's all messed up. Not that it's entirely bad, but do you ever remember high school being like this?"

"It's kind of nice," said Peter. "Everyone is getting a date to the dance."

Laura winced, and Peter instantly regretted his remark. "No, I mean, there's you . . . you still have time. Oh, Laura, I'm sorry. Listen, I'll talk to some of the guys and—"

"No!" she yelled, backing away from him. "No more matchmaking!" Unsure why she was so mad at him—when it wasn't *his* fault—Laura turned and scurried away from her old friend.

"Laura!" he called after her, but she didn't stop.

As if this day could be any more wonderful, Laura found a police car parked in her driveway when she reached home. Instantly she lifted the duffel bag and clutched it tightly to her chest; she could almost feel the tingle of danger coming from the magic bow, and she knew it was threatened. As she slowly walked toward the front door, it opened, and her father escorted a uniformed police officer out.

"I think that's all we need," said the officer, closing her notebook.

"Oh, here's my daughter," said Ed Sweeney, pointing to Laura. "The house is okay, honey, but it's quite a mess. We had a break-in."

"Oh, no!" exclaimed Laura. She tried to look more surprised than she felt. "Did they . . . did they take anything?"

"Oddly, not much," answered her father with a puzzled expression. "Some of your mom's jewelry had been lying out, and they took that, but they left a lot of electronics and appliances and stuff."

The police officer gazed suspiciously at Laura. "It looks like they tossed your bedroom worse than the others. Do you have any idea what they were searching for?"

"No!" She gave a nervous laugh.

"What's in the bag?" asked the officer.

"Just my books . . . and a prop for the school play." Laura began to open the bag.

"That's all right," said her father, looking a bit annoyed with the police officer. "My daughter is a straight-A student who's never been in any kind of trouble. She can't have anything to do with this."

"All right," said the officer. "Take an inventory, then let me and your insurance company know exactly what they took. You might want to put in a burglar alarm when you fix that broken window in back."

"We probably will," he agreed. "Thanks for coming so quickly, Officer."

"That's my job." The police officer tipped her hat and returned to her patrol car.

In shock, Laura watched the officer drive away, and her father put his arm around her shoulders. "Hon, don't let the questions bother you—it's not your fault. We've got lots of cleaning up to do. Why don't you start with your bedroom, and I'll work downstairs."

But it is *my fault,* Laura wanted to shout. *I have a magical bow, and villains are trying to steal it!* She wanted to tell her father the truth so badly, but she knew she would have to use the bow in order to prove it. And she didn't want to do that again.

"I don't feel very well," she said, already planning to stay home tomorrow to protect the precious bow.

He frowned. "Seeing your room won't make you feel any better."

Glumly Laura climbed the stairs and stepped cautiously into her bedroom. When she saw the ripped pillows, torn mattress, overturned dressers, broken lamps, and scattered papers, she began to cry. Her most private possessions were scattered all over the floor, and she felt violated. It didn't bring any comfort that she still had the object they were looking for, because the bow had done nothing but make her life miserable.

I ought to just give it to them, she reflected. But Laura couldn't stand to think what Madame Luisa would do with such a powerful weapon. It made her shiver with fright.

I ought to destroy it, she thought. She could burn the stupid bow in the fireplace, but she worried that she needed it to reverse the spells. Besides, it was an artifact from a magical time three thousand years ago, and destroying it was like destroying one of the wonders of the universe.

Unsure what to do, Laura sat on her shredded bed and cried.

Eleven

Laura Sweeney didn't go to school for a week. Since she almost never missed school unless she was deathly ill, her parents barely questioned it. After a while they took her to the doctor, and he couldn't find much wrong with her. But there was a low-grade fever going around, and Laura was careful to keep the thermometer no higher than a hundred when she heated it on the light bulb.

There was a lot of straightening to do at the house, and workers came to fix the window and measure for a burglar alarm, which would be installed next week. Still Laura didn't feel entirely safe sitting home all alone while her mom and dad were at work. She did more cleaning than a sick person really ought to do, and maybe that was another reason her parents didn't complain. Her mom made sure she got her schoolwork assignments from her friends.

Taryn came over often, but she was depressing with her talk of Chester, the Homecoming Dance, and the dresses they were all going to wear. Laura tried to act enthusiastic for her friend, but she was afraid she didn't fake it very well. She kept hoping and dreading that Peter would come over to visit, but he never did.

According to Taryn, Megan was keeping a short leash on Peter, especially after it became known that he had talked to Laura in the hallway. He had also broken Cupidity's edict not to socialize with Laura, and Cupidity and Megan were best buds now. Laura considered just leaving the mismatched couples alone, but she felt personally responsible for Cupidity. Plus she didn't believe Peter was happy with Megan, and he seemed honestly torn.

The question is, can I battle the perfect cheerleader to win Peter's heart—even when they share a love spell? Laura didn't know the answer, and it was easier lying in bed thinking than taking any kind of action.

What kept her alert was the certainty that Madame Luisa and Arnie were out there somewhere, waiting for her to let down her guard. Twice in one day she thought she saw a white van cruising slowly past her house, and her phone rang with constant hang-ups.

By Thursday she had decided that sitting in the house, guarding the Cupidity Stupidity bow, was driving her crazy. And it wasn't doing anyone any good. *I've got to do something,* she realized. *The dance is only eight days away.*

It was time to stop being scared and go back on the offensive. No one else knew about the magical weapon, except Cupidity, who had forgotten what she knew about it. *How can I free the love zombies?* Laura wondered. *Who could help me?*

Cupidity's father, came the answer. Although she had met him only once, she had a feeling that he knew more about his strange daughter than he had let on. But how could she contact him when he lived in California? Maybe there was a phone number or an address in Cupidity's apartment.

Laura collected all the arrows she had hidden around the house and put them into the duffel bag with the bow. Carrying her prize, she headed outside. She didn't have a car, so she had to walk to Cupidity's apartment—but she had plenty of energy for that. The new girl would be in school this time of day, and Laura would have to break into her apartment. She wondered if she would have the courage to do so.

After half an hour of brisk walking, taking alleys and side streets, Laura stood outside Cupidity's luxury apartment complex. In the middle of a chilly September afternoon, most of the residents were at work or school. Dried leaves skittered across the sidewalk, and the trees waved their bare, skeletal branches at the slate sky.

The gloom matched Laura's mood, and she nearly turned away from Cupidity's door. If she had to break in she might get into more trouble. Then she decided that more trouble was barely possible, so Laura took a deep breath and tried to buck up her own spirits.

Come on, girl, you've dreamed all your life about the great heroes and fools in Greco-Roman mythology, and now it's happening in real life! Think of this as a play starring you. The only problem is, you don't know whether it's a tragedy or a comedy. . . .

On impulse, she reached for the doorknob and turned it, and the door creaked open. Laura jerked in surprise, but she knew that lots of people in Denton left their front doors unlocked. Plus Cupidity was a ditz—and getting ditzier every lovesick minute. She hefted her duffel bag, pushed open the door, and stepped into the empty apartment.

"Whoa," muttered Laura. The place had none of the elegance she had seen before. Now it looked like a teenager's bedroom, with posters of rock stars, Mardi Gras beads, stickers, and other knickknacks covering the walls. Notes and papers lay scattered across the floor, and dirty plates and fast-food wrappers covered the tables. It was obvious that Cupidity had stopped keeping house after getting amnesia.

As she kicked a mass of papers out of her way, her spirits sank. There was no way she was going to find anything helpful in this mess. If she wanted to be nasty, Laura figured she could always turn Cupidity over to the authorities as a minor living alone, but that would only cause trouble. It certainly wouldn't do anything to free Peter and the others, and it wouldn't free her from the burden of what was in the duffel bag.

Laura heard shuffling behind her, and she realized that she wasn't alone. She was about to reach into the bag for her weapon when a voice said, "That won't be necessary, Laura."

She whirled around and saw Cupidity's dapper but frail father, looking rather disgusted at his surroundings. "Apparently we both came to the simultaneous conclusion that something had to be done," he said, removing an elegant silk glove from his hand.

Laura stammered, "I, uh . . . do you know . . . there's something in this bag. How much do you know about your daughter?"

"Too much." The elderly man gave her

a sour frown and looked down at the duffel bag in her hands. "Do you know you're the first mortal to have used that bow? And you say it's been working for you?"

In shock, she nodded.

"Remarkable. All these years, we never really needed that obnoxious cherub. I'm not his father, and I couldn't tell you who is." The elder held out his ungloved hand. "My name is Mercury, the messenger god."

Laura felt herself swooning, and she looked down at his elegant wing-tipped shoes. Like ghostly banners, real wings seem to sprout from his heels, and Laura fell backward. His outstretched hand caught her, and his strength was effortless as he steadied her.

"You're . . . you're a Roman god?" she asked, sounding more doubtful than she felt.

He sighed. "I know you haven't seen many shrines to me lately, but I used to be quite the rage."

"And you're not Cupidity's dad?"

"Cupidity is Cupid in disguise," he answered with a frown. "And now he's madly in love with a skater boy, thanks to you."

Laura's face brightened with hope. "Is this like old Greek dramas where the god shows up to fix things? *Deus ex machina?*"

"No!" he snapped. "This is reality. I suppose I could take that bow from you and make matters worse—like you did—but I can't fix love problems."

"Who can?" asked Laura desperately.

"Cupid's mother," said the god, thin-lipped. "Venus."

Laura moved toward the door. "Well then, let's go get her. Come on! You're the messenger god—send her a message!"

Mercury lifted his white eyebrows. "It won't be that easy. Venus doesn't live with the rest of us. She can be difficult to approach, and frankly, none of the gods want to deal with her. *You* will have to approach her."

"Me?" asked Laura in shock. "That doesn't seem very fair. Isn't she your sister or something?"

Mercury pursed his lips and replied, "It is eminently fair since it was you who involved the gods in the first place. Don't you remember calling on Jupiter to bring you a boyfriend?"

Laura wracked her brain and finally remembered back to that rainy night after the first day of school. She gasped. "Whoa there! I said that one night, yes, but I thought it was like a . . . rhetorical request."

"Well, we didn't take it that way," sniffed Mercury. "We're very passé, not a lot of people believe in us anymore. Not like the olden days when Julius Caesar's battle cry was 'Venus Victrix!' He never would have gotten so far without her help. Ah well, I guess this Cupidity affair just proves that we're old and useless."

"That's a little harsh," replied Laura, touching the old man's arm. She blinked at him in realization. "You mean, you sent Cupid in disguise to help *me* get a boyfriend?"

Mercury sighed. "Yes, Cupid wanted to get to know you as a friend . . . to know who was best for you."

"Wow," murmured Laura, "he sure screwed up."

The old man grabbed the duffel bag and shook it angrily. "You didn't help matters by piercing Cupid with one of his own arrows! Since you started this, you must end it. You must be the one to come to Los Angeles and approach Venus."

Laura gulped and pushed back her glasses. "How tough can that be?"

"Let's put it this way," said Mercury, "Venus has tamed all her boyfriends, including the Minotaur. And she doesn't know anything about Cupid's assignment, because we were afraid to tell her."

"Uh-oh." Laura began to wring her hands. "You know, I can't just like . . . fly off to Los Angeles. I have a mom and dad, and these two creeps are trying to steal Cupid's bow."

"I'll take care of them," promised Mercury as he handed her back the duffel bag with the precious cargo. "You have the power to distract your parents. They won't even remember they have a daughter." He pointed to the duffel bag.

Laura felt the curve of the bow in her hand and winced in disgust. "Use it on my own parents?"

"It's for a good cause," said Mercury, "and you don't have much time."

"What do you mean, I don't have much time?"

The elegant elder paced the floor, kicking the wrappers and papers with his wingtips. "Cupid will soon lose his disguise—no more Cupidity. I see he's been partying as usual."

"Probably more than usual," answered Laura, "considering who he's with. Will changing back cure his amnesia?"

Mercury shook his head. "I don't know, but his disguise lasts only twenty-five days. It is over at midnight a week from tomorrow."

Laura's eyes widened in horror. "That's the night of the Homecoming Dance, and she'll be there with Cody. *He'll* be there . . . whatever. You're right, I don't have much time."

"We will have to find Venus first," said Mercury with a sigh, "and I will have to get approval for all of this from Jupiter. I don't see how he can turn down a brave mortal who is willing to seek Venus on his behalf." The dapper god looked intently at her. "You are willing, aren't you?"

Laura nodded, unable to speak. *I do seem to be the starstruck heroine of this drama,* she thought. *And somehow I've become the fill-in Cupid while the real one is out sick.*

Mercury lifted a well-manicured finger. "Be ready at midnight Saturday night, and I'll come for you. I can't do much about love, but I'm fairly good at transportation. Don't worry about luggage, we'll supply what you need. Bring the bow, as having that will get Venus's attention."

Mercury gave Laura a wrinkled smile. "Do take care of your parents first—try giving them a *romantic* gift, if you know what I mean. I'll see you Saturday night."

He tipped his hat and strolled out the front door, as Laura gripped the bow through the heavy nylon of the bag. Now all of her questions had been answered; like the heroes of most Greek tragedy, she was in the middle of a mess of her own making. Numbly Laura walked toward the door and decided, *I've got one more place to go.*

Through binoculars Laura could watch all the happy couples filing out of Fimbrey High School from her hiding spot behind a telephone pole on the far side of the parking lot. Despite the distance, she could see Megan and Peter, holding hands and joking with Cupidity and Cody. Behind them came Emma and Jake; Jake was wearing dark gray instead of his usual pastel collared shirts, and Emma had on a cardigan sweater.

Laura lowered the binoculars and rubbed her eyes, but she soon went back to spying. It was getting colder, and Cupidity had actually pulled the top up on her convertible. The golden couples didn't linger long in the chilly parking lot, but she could imagine them making plans to meet later. Peter looked happy with his cheerleader, although she caught him glancing over his shoulder in her direction. She knew he couldn't see her, but it was still eerie.

Finally Laura spotted the person she really wanted to see—Taryn, accompanied by her man, Chester. Were they genuine, or had they been smitten, too, by the magical arrows? It was impossible to tell fake Cupid love from real love, although it was clear that some social barriers had broken down. She had the means to break down more of them—think of the havoc she could wreak among this crowd of unsuspecting students.

Laura found that she was gripping the bow through the nylon of the duffel bag. She took her hands off the curved weapon and let it fall back into the bag, and the impulse to shoot it went away. *It's hard to have power and not abuse it,* she thought.

Fortunately, Chester and Taryn were walking downtown, where Chester had to do some youth program as part of his probation, and Laura was able to ambush them on the sidewalk, away from prying eyes. Gripping the duffel bag, Laura dashed across the sidewalk. "Taryn, can I talk to you?" she asked.

"Oh, Laura!" said her friend happily. She took off her backpack and unzipped it. "I was going to come over to your house later this afternoon. I've got the assignments in calculus and English—"

Laura held out a hand to stop her. "Just hang on to them for me." She smiled at the hulking boy, whose brawny arm engulfed Taryn's shoulders. "Chester, can I talk to her alone for just a second? I promise, I won't keep her long."

"Sure," he said, nodding and stepping

away. "I heard you been sick. How ya feelin'?"

"Terrible," she answered, mustering a smile. "But I'm happy for the two of you guys."

"Thanks." Chester spotted one of his buddies and waved to him. "You know, Laura, if you need a date to that dance—"

Wincing, she responded, "I appreciate the offer, but I think I'm going to be out of town."

When Chester finally turned his back to them and lumbered toward his friends, Taryn asked, "What's the matter with you? You don't look sick. Insane maybe, but not sick."

"I'm not sick," Laura admitted, "and I am going out of town for a few days. I want you to cover for me."

Taryn stared at her. "How?"

"It won't be difficult," explained Laura. "As far as the school goes, I'm already absent. There's a good chance my parents will never call you to check on me, but if they do, just say I'll call them later. They'll forget all about it."

Taryn looked skeptical. "Are we talking

about *your* parents? You didn't trade them in for Cupidity's parents, did you?"

Laura looked intently at her friend and held her hand. "Just trust me on this. It's all going to be okay."

"*What's* going to be okay?" asked Taryn in frustration. "Where are you going? For how long? *Why?*"

"I don't know," admitted Laura. "But it's urgent that I go, believe me." Desperately, she began to back away from her best friend. "I'll call your cell phone."

Worriedly, Taryn followed her. "Are you in some kind of trouble? Does this have anything to do with the Conjure Woman?"

"Stay away from her!" warned Laura. She gripped her duffel bag and hurried off down the street.

Five minutes before midnight on Saturday, Laura stood in her parents' bedroom, silhouetted in the light from the hallway. The Sweeneys were snoring a few feet away, blissfully unaware that their loving daughter was aiming a bow and arrow at them. *This is too easy,* she thought.

Before she plunged two people who'd been married for twenty-two years into passionate love, Laura made sure they would find her handwritten note on the vanity. The note "reminded" them that she was spending a few days at Taryn's house to catch up on her schoolwork before going back to school. She doubted if they would spend much time worrying about her after she fixed them.

Holding her breath as she always did, Laura shot a love sticker into the first sleeping figure. Her mom groaned softly from the wound as Laura rummaged in the duffel bag for a second arrow. She had never stopped to count the arrows, but it seemed as if there was always one at hand when she needed it. Before the groaning could wake her dad, she stuck him with an arrow too. Now they were moaning in unison, and she sure wanted to be out of the bedroom before they woke up.

As she walked down the stairs she saw a dapper man in a homburg standing at the bottom of the staircase. The elderly god tipped his hat as she approached. "Ready to go, Miss Sweeney?"

"I guess so," she answered doubtfully. "I'm just wearing this sweater and jeans, but you said I didn't need a lot of clothes. What about a toothbrush?"

"You've got the bow, that's all the luggage you need." Mercury snapped his fingers, and the living room of the Sweeney home was filled with two massive, sparkling wheels. As Laura stared in amazement the colorful apparition solidified into a gleaming chariot encrusted with jewels and golden inlay. The reins glowed like rays of the sun, and they stretched from the shining coach to two winged horses. The ghostly steeds pranced on the carpet, anxious to be going, and Laura staggered on her feet.

Mercury grabbed her elbow and steadied her. With a smile he said, "To begin with, Cupidity was on a quest. Now it's *you* on the quest. So I figured you should go in style. Welcome aboard Apollo's chariot—the original one."

The elegant god helped her onto the gleaming coach, and the ethereal steeds snorted their approval. Laura felt the vehicle shifting under her feet, as if it were real, and she gripped her duffel bag and the rail for support. Mercury took his place beside her, and he picked up the golden reins. Laura panicked, thinking they were about to slam into the wall. But this magical conveyance had gotten into the house, so there must be a way to get it out.

"Hang on!" said Mercury, snapping the reins. At once the horses reared and the carriage took off, zipping through the front wall of the house as if it weren't there. As a lonely bell tower chimed midnight in the town of Denton, Ohio, Apollo's twinkling chariot rose above the rooftops and shot into the stars.

Twelve

Laura stirred from a very deep sleep, and she felt the soft contours of her bed and the warmth of her blankets wrapping her like a cocoon. *Oh, what a crazy, delirious dream,* she thought. *One for the record books, no doubt inspired by reading too much mythology.*

In her rococo nightmare, Cupid had come to Fimbrey as a high school student, and Peter was dating Megan! Everything was turned upside down. *I'll have to cut out the Roman gods for a while,* she decided, *at least after eating a whole pizza.*

Her stomach felt tied in knots, and her memory was very cloudy. Laura wondered what time it was, and she noted that it was dark in her bedroom. She couldn't see a thing, but she could hear the drone of traffic outside. That meant it had to be later than it seemed, because she didn't normally hear much traffic in the middle of the night.

The days are growing shorter, thought Laura as she sat up in bed and rubbed her eyes. She looked for her slippers on the floor by her bed but couldn't find them, and that's when she decided to turn on the light. Her hand fumbled for the lamp on her nightstand, because it wasn't where it was supposed to be. Her fingers finally found the knob near the base and twisted it, and the room was illuminated.

"Whaaa!" she screamed when she saw unfamiliar paintings and luxurious chaise longues. Laura dove back under the covers and pulled them around her shivering body, until she realized she was still wearing her clothes. The sweater, the jeans, the strange bedroom . . . and the duffel bag on the floor.

Whoa! she thought, sitting up again, *it isn't a dream!* She looked more closely at the room and realized that the French doors led to a balcony, and beyond that there was a huge, sprawling city. It was lit up like the glowing chariot . . . the one from her dream.

A door whispered open, and she turned to see an elegant older man, who nodded to her. "I'm glad to see you're awake."

"Mercury!" she exclaimed with a gasp.

"And still have your mind," he added. "You passed out on the way here. I thought we were going to lose you over Kansas."

She blinked at him. "How long have I been asleep?"

"We left Ohio early Sunday morning, and it's now Monday morning," he answered. "Over twenty-four hours you've slept. I'm sorry, I had forgotten what effect travel by sky chariot has on mortals. As I told you, we're rather rusty at this."

"It's okay," she answered numbly. "I remember it all now . . . we've got to find Venus."

"We'll try." Mercury sighed and sat in one of the luxurious chairs. "I looked in the moratorium—do you know what that is?"

Laura nodded. "Like a crystal ball, only it's a bowl of water."

"Yes," he answered, "but Venus knows how to cloud the image. I thought I saw a hotel, which is why I brought you here. This is a hotel in Beverly Hills where she often stays when she's recovering from plastic surgery or liposuction."

"Liposuction?" asked Laura with distaste. "What is she, like three thousand years old?"

Mercury rolled his eyes. "Yes, and she needs lots of help to keep looking beautiful. I thought we might get lucky, but she's not here."

"Who would know where she is?"

The dapper god gazed at his manicured fingers for a moment and seemed to be thinking. "There are a few she trusts . . . her posse, as you would call it."

"Let's find them." Laura started toward the door, energized by her determination to set things right.

Mercury cleared his throat, and the girl stopped in mid-stride, knowing it was going to be bad news. "There's just one problem," said the god. "Her posse is all satyrs."

"Satyrs?" she asked with a squeak in her

voice. "You mean . . . like randy goatmen?"

"Yes," he answered gravely. "Randy goatmen, and age hasn't tempered them much. Dionysius and Cupid also hang with her, when they feel like it."

With a groan the elder rose to his feet. "Perhaps we should check all the hotels in Los Angeles first."

"Oh, come on, it can't be that bad," insisted Laura. "The posse, I mean."

"Venus has some local haunts we should check," said Mercury. "I'm certain about the hotel I saw in my vision, but I don't know which one it is."

When Laura started out the door, he gripped her arm and pointed to the duffel bag. "Don't forget the bow and arrows— that's your passport into my world."

For two days Laura Sweeney and Mercury roamed Los Angeles in a Rolls-Royce limousine piloted by a burly driver named Lar. Laura recalled that Roman households often had their own domestic gods, who were called the Lares, and she wondered if Lar was one of them. She had a lot of time to ponder this question, since they visited every plastic surgeon, luxury spa, private club, and fancy hotel in town. But they found no sign of Venus under any of her pseudonyms.

Laura's senses were blown by all the wonders she had seen in the city—museums to massage parlors—but they weren't getting any closer to their goal. Nobody had seen Venus, who had several human guises and identities. After questioning so many people, Laura felt as if she were part of some surreal TV cop show. As they cruised a street north of town, night began to fall on another day of frustration.

They stopped at a busy corner on a main boulevard, and Mercury leaned over to whisper something to their driver. Yawning, Laura gazed out the window and saw what looked like a pleasant residence hotel on the corner. The sign read MOUNT OLYMPUS RETIREMENT HOME.

She chuckled and pointed. "Look, there's a place we ought to check, Mount Olympus."

"Venus never visits the old gang," answered Lar sadly.

Realization dawned on Laura as her

gaze traveled from the driver to the messenger god. "Is that where you live? Now I remember—Cupidity said something about a retirement home."

"Yes, that's our home," answered the elder, sounding tired and frail.

"Can I see it, and meet the rest of you?"

Mercury gave her a crinkled smile. "No, you don't want to meet us. You should think of us as we exist in the old books and stories, not as we are now. Our time is past, and this fiasco only proves it."

Laura suddenly felt very sorry for the aged immortal and his forgotten kind, who had only wanted to do a favor for a girl they didn't even know. "You're so close to home, why don't you spend the night here?" she suggested. "And tell me where to find the satyrs, because time is running out."

The elder nodded thoughtfully. "I suppose it is the moment when you prove yourself. If you're successful and find Venus, tell Lar to call me. I would go with you, but the leader of the satyrs is Pan, who is my son. We don't speak anymore, I'm afraid."

"Oh," said Laura sympathetically. "I

hope I'm still speaking to my parents after this."

Mercury assured her, "While you continue the search, I'll go back to Ohio and make sure you aren't missed."

"Excuse me, sir," said Lar, "but I heard on Dionysius's grapevine that the gang is at Pinkie's Pool Parlor, looking for Cupid."

"All right, take her there, Lar," said Mercury. "She'll have better luck with them than I would. I'm going home."

"Very good, sir." Lar parked the limousine in front of the retirement home and rushed to open the passenger door for Mercury.

"Pinkie's Pool Parlor?" asked Laura hesitantly.

"That's where we would be looking for Cue," answered Lar with a smile.

"Tell Pan . . . tell him I'm sorry I wasn't a better father," said Mercury hesitantly. "His mother and I had too many differences. See you tomorrow, I hope." Lar helped the frail god out of the Rolls-Royce and escorted him to the door.

A moment later, the chauffeur returned and said, "That was very noble of you, my lady, to let him rest. He's always cared more for humans than any of the rest of them. Just hold your own with the satyrs, my lady, and don't take any guff."

Laura nodded, with a sick feeling in her stomach. When she pressed the button and rolled down the window, the odor of salt, sea foam, and hibiscus invaded her senses. Giant cypress and pine trees waving in the cool evening wind told Laura that the landscape was changing. Through her haze of disappointment she realized that she was on a fantastic adventure, carrying a magical weapon. Someday they would make movies about her!

I'd settle for a date to Homecoming, she decided, just before falling asleep in the gently rocking vehicle.

Laura awoke when the heavy car bounced over a rut in the road, and she bolted upright with a start. She looked around to see a drab street that was barely lit by a few orange streetlights. Most of the storefronts were empty, but a few showed signs of life, especially the flickering neon that spelled out PINKIE'S POOL PARLOR. A fleet of big-hog motorcycles were parked in front of the establishment. In the driver's seat, Lar hummed softly to himself as if nothing was amiss.

She gulped. "That's where we're going?"

"Where *you're* going," he answered. "I'm going to stay out here, unless I hear you scream."

"Satyrs?" she muttered fearfully. "Open the trunk and let me get my bow."

"That's the spirit!" answered Lar, sounding relieved. He popped the trunk lid, and Laura climbed into the breezy night. This grungy patch of urban blight hardly seemed like cheerful southern California anymore, but she didn't think they had driven that far. Laura grabbed the familiar duffel bag and slammed the trunk shut.

Even before she got to the door, she heard raucous male laughter and loud rock music. When she opened the door, the music became louder and sounded very foreign, with lots of flutes and bongo drums. With a start, she realized that it was *live* music, being played by what looked like a country and western band. On stage were several shaggy cowboys, wearing cowboy boots and chaps. Two of them were playing pan pipes—reeds of different lengths tied together—two played drums, and the fifth played a ukulele.

They were wrapped up in their playing, so Laura strode down between the pool tables until she was close enough that they had to see her. That was when she noticed that the musicians weren't wearing chaps over their cowboy boots—those were gigantic hooves at the ends of their hairy legs!

They gave the song a rollicking finish, then set down their instruments and stared at Laura. One satyr smiled, and his mischievous green eyes twinkled. A dark one seemed to lick his lips, and another one lifted a mug and toasted her. She quickly reached into the duffel bag and took out the bow and arrows. *I have to show them, anyway,* she decided.

The one with the green eyes laughed. "Oh, look, isn't that cute. She's come with a darling little weapon!"

The satyr rose to his hooves and stalked toward her. His tight T-shirt didn't do much to hide his silver-gray pelt, and she could see that his upper torso was well muscled. Below the waist, he was a goat. "I'm sorry, dearie, but you missed the party," he said with a bow. "However, visitors like you are always welcome."

The other satyrs laughed and stared lustfully at her, and Laura lifted the bow and took aim at each one in turn. The elder creature kept circling her, and he said, "That toy is not going to hurt us."

"I think it will," answered Laura with determination. "It's *Cupid's* bow, and I know how to use it!"

That brought the silver-haired satyr to a halt, and it made the others stop laughing. "Don't come any closer, but take a good look at it," ordered Laura, thrusting the bow into the light over a pool table. The weapon tingled in her hands as if it were especially eager to inflict love misery on these creatures of the woods and the cue stick.

"By Hades, that *is* his bow," said a drummer, who still had some dark hair in his pelt. "Pan, be careful there. I like you, but not *that* much."

"Understood," said the gray beard. "Why should I believe any of this?"

Laura lifted her chin and blurted, "Because I've been hanging out with your father. Nice fellow, great dresser—dig those wingtips. Hey, he's sorry he wasn't a better father to you, but I guess he couldn't get along with your mother." She wanted to ask what species his mother was, but she dared not.

The satyr blinked at her in amazement and acted as if he had just been shot with Cupid's arrow. After a moment, he scratched one of the horns that poked up through his silvery mane and asked, "Is Cupid in danger?"

"Yes, he's in Denton, Ohio!" she answered, as if that explained it all.

As the satyrs muttered among themselves in a language she couldn't understand, Laura lessened her tension on the bowstring. "Listen, Cupid is not in physical danger, but he has amnesia. He's not in his right mind."

"Oh!" roared the satyr with the ukelele. "Then he's perfectly normal." One drummer laughed, but Pan did not.

"Would I have his bow if he was normal?" asked Laura in desperation. "Listen, I only want to know where Venus is. Tell me where to find her, and I'll go away."

"Ah," said Pan, stroking his belly as he stepped to her right, "we can't give away our friend's position to the enemy, now can we?"

She lifted the bow, pulled back the string, and took aim at his sculpted but hairy chest. "Take one more step, and you'll be a monogamous satyr. I've already done Cupidity, and I can take care of you, too."

"Who did you say?" asked Pan, halting his effort to outflank her. "Who's Cupidity?"

"Cupid . . . now that she's a girl. Vulcan put her in a disguise—a really hot disguise."

"Oooh, gossip!" they cried. "Tell! Do tell!"

At their delighted smirks, Laura sighed. "All right, settle down, and I'll tell you the whole story. But no satyr stuff near me. Okay?"

As soon as Pan had heard Laura's story, including parts where he laughed hysterically, he jumped to his feet and rallied his band of satyrs. "Everybody! Listen up—get your leathers on. We're taking a cross-country bike ride!"

"Yahoo!" cheered the satyrs, stomping around on their big hooves in the empty poolroom. "I want the three-wheeler!" cried one of them, dashing out of the encampment.

"Wait a minute!" yelled Laura, "Are we talking motorcycles? I don't want to go on a cross-anything ride—"

"Do you want to find Venus?" asked Pan, cutting her off. He lowered his voice to add, "I know where she'll be on Friday, but I can't tell a mortal like you. Still, if I feel like going on a trip and inviting you along, who's to know? It was an accident, right? If we leave now, we can make it by Friday, and I think we'll end up close to Ohio."

Laura gnawed her lower lip. "Finding her on Friday will be cutting it awfully close to the dance."

"Just think how much time you'll save having us with you." The silver-haired satyr winked at her and added, "When we put our leathers on, we'll look like any regular motorcycle gang. Don't we clean up real nice, boys?"

"Yeah! Sure do!" growled the randy goatmen.

"All right," relented Laura. If they didn't know where Venus was until Friday, she had time to kill . . . if she could trust them.

Ignoring her, the crew of five satyrs began to don oversized boots, leather pants, leather jackets, bandannas, and scuffed helmets. Soon they were transformed into an especially scruffy gang of motorcyclists.

They gave Laura a helmet and her own sleek leathers, which fit perfectly. After she strapped the bow to her back, she looked at herself in the bathroom mirror, thinking, *I actually look hot for once in my life.*

"Let's ride!" yelled Pan, heading for the door. Whooping and hollering, his gang of satyrs stumbled after him. They leaped on their big hogs, and started the engines with lusty roars and clouds of greasy smoke.

Pan turned to Laura and pointed to the rest of the banana seat behind him, then held out his hand.

I agreed to do this—no excuses, she thought. With a terrified squeak, Laura grabbed his hand and climbed onto the back of the big two-wheeler.

"Hold on!" shouted Lar, the chauffeur.

He dashed in front of the motorcycles, waving his hands. "You boys will behave yourselves with Miss Sweeney, I hope!"

"She's under my father's protection," declared Pan. He zipped up his aged leather jacket, which was covered in road rash, and added, "She'll be safer with us than with you and Pops. You don't know the kind of place we're going."

Laura shouted doubtfully, "I'll be fine!"

"I'll get word to Mercury," answered Lar.

Pan revved his engine until it sounded like Jupiter's thunder, and the chauffeur scurried out of the way. When the satyr waved his arm, the growl of engines reached a fevered pitch. Laura heard the click of the gears, and she gripped Pan's waist as the chopper flew off the curb and shot into the night.

Thirteen

"Yes, yes, Mr. Sweeney, this is Taryn's father," said Mercury, who was seated in an unmarked, high-tech van parked across the street from Taryn's house. He and his crew of expensive minions were intercepting any calls between the two households, although so far there had only been two. "I know I don't sound like myself, but I have a cold." The god gave a polite cough.

On the other end of the line, Edward Sweeney stammered, "It's . . . it's just that we haven't seen our daughter since last Saturday or Sunday. I'm not sure when." He added quickly, "I've been very busy."

"I'm sure you have," answered Mercury

with only a trace of sarcasm. "I can tell you that Laura has been a total delight to me and—"

He paused to look at a technician, who read off a computer screen, "Melissa."

"Melissa," said Mercury. "Yes, Melissa really likes Laura, who is a delightful houseguest. I think Taryn has brought her up to speed on her schoolwork, and she'll return home at the end of the week. Now don't you worry about Laura . . . just get back to those pressing matters of yours. Good-bye."

"Good-bye." As Ed Sweeney's voice faded away, Mercury heard him plead, "Honey, wait until I get off the phone!"

The messenger god sighed and took off the headset. "Well, that should hold them for a while. It's Wednesday night, only two days to go. I think you gentlemen can spare me for a while." He started to open the door of the van.

"Boss, do you want us to drive you somewhere?" asked the technician.

"No, I can walk there," he replied. "It's something I have to do alone."

Grabbing his cane, the elder got out of

the van and walked gingerly down the damp sidewalk. It was October, and the chill winds of Janus were in the air. He longed for the warm, sun-kissed shores of California, Greece, or Italy, but he had promised to help Laura Sweeney. It was probably hopeless to appeal to Venus, but Laura had been able to move the gods to action before.

Mercury had also returned to Denton because he felt a responsibility to Cupid. They had sent the inept cherub on this quest, knowing that meddling in the affairs of mortals was dangerous. This was another instance where they should have minded their own business instead of getting caught up in crazy schemes. Whether Venus made it or not, Mercury felt obligated to be there at the dance . . . when it would all unravel.

Unless he could persuade Cupidity not to go.

By the time the aged god reached her apartment complex, night had fallen in all its dark glory upon the quiet Ohio town. Autumn had arrived, and it felt like olden times knowing there was a fall festival coming on Friday. Now was the time to shelter the harvest and loved ones to make ready for the icy grip of winter.

Mercury walked slowly up the steps to Cupidity's door, and he could hear laughter and raucous music coming from within. *Her neighbors must love her,* he thought sarcastically. Since it was technically his abode, he didn't knock; he just barged in.

He caught Cupidity and Cody kissing, or maybe they were dancing, in the middle of the heavily littered living room. Rock music was blaring so loudly that they couldn't hear him come in, but a gust of wind entered with the messenger god.

"Cupidity, look at this mess!" he yelled at her. "You haven't been doing your chores."

She pulled away from Cody and looked sheepishly at him. "No, I suppose I haven't been. Why the visit, Dad?"

"Because I ought to live here," he answered. "With you. How can I desert my only child . . . and miss out on you growing up?"

Cody shifted uncomfortably on his feet. "Excuse me, Mister, uh . . . Cupidity's dad, but I can look after your daughter for you. I'm over here every minute."

"Yes, you're all over her," muttered the angry "father," slamming the door behind him. "Young lady, because you've made the house such a mess—while entertaining boys without my permission—I'm going to ground you! You can't go anywhere until . . . Saturday."

"No!" she shrieked. "The Homecoming Dance is Friday. I've got my dress, my date . . . we're going with a bunch of people. You can't do this to me, Papa!"

"Please, Mister, have a heart," insisted Cody. "We'll clean it up, we'll start right now. Hey, Cupie, where's the number for that maid service?"

"You'll be leaving right now, Mr. Kenyon," insisted Mercury, mustering all the strength he had and shoving the handsome lad toward the door. "You've had it your own way, but now Daddy's home."

Thankfully, the boy was too dazed to resist, and Mercury managed to shove him outside and lock the door behind him. Cody cursed and beat on the door a few times, while Cupidity pouted. Mercury caught his breath, because the disguised cherub was truly the masterwork of Vulcan's art. It was a pity that this dazzling creature was not going to last until the end of the week.

"This . . . this is the worst thing you've ever done!" wailed Cupidity.

"Oh, come on," said her fake father sternly. "I've grounded you lots of times, and you never carried on like this."

She gazed at him with a troubled frown, and he knew that Laura had been right—the cherub had truly lost all memory, except for the cover story that went with the disguise, which she thought was real.

"This feels worse," complained the petite blond, stamping her foot on the hamburger wrappers. "I want to be Homecoming Queen more than anything I've ever wanted in my whole life! Come on, Papa, you can't just pop into my life and stop me."

"I can try," he vowed.

More pounding shook the door, and Cody's forlorn voice shouted, "I'll call you later, Cupie!"

"I love you, Codykins!" she cried in anguish.

★

The satyrs never got tired. They could go for twenty-four hours, day and night, never stopping . . . just riding those big two-wheelers down the interstate. It was a good thing Laura was young and had already gotten lots of sleep in her youthful life, because she didn't get any sleep on their mad dash across the country. She took some solace from the fact that they were headed in the right direction and got closer to Ohio with every blurred mile.

The pain set in only when she got off the banana seat and tried to walk after hours frozen in place behind Pan. She made the motorcyclists stop as often as she could without being a nuisance, because she knew time was running out.

It was late on Friday afternoon when they stopped someplace in Indiana. The town looked so much like Ohio that she got homesick, although she didn't remember the hotel chain. Why had they stopped at this podunk hotel? Laura couldn't shake the thought that maybe the satyrs were taking her for a ride—figuratively as well as literally. Maybe there was no Venus at the end of the road, just a Homecoming Dance to which she wasn't invited.

She looked up to see Pan walking toward her with a big smile on his face. "We're here," he said proudly.

"Here?" she asked, glancing at the tree-lined street in the quiet midwestern town, much like the one she had left. "Venus is *here?*"

The silver-haired satyr pointed to the nondescript, mid-sized hotel. "It's Friday, so she'll check in sometime tonight. Come, I'll show you."

He took off his battered helmet, and she gasped. "Listen, you'd better put that back on—I can see your horns."

"It doesn't matter here." The satyr waved to her and strode toward the hotel, walking with a swagger in his specially designed boots.

Laura groaned as she stretched her stiff legs, but she managed to follow him into the hotel. After the elegant L.A. hotels and spas she had visited, this couldn't be where Venus was hanging out. No way was this mediocre roadside inn the grand hotel in Mercury's vision.

When they stepped into the lobby, she saw why Pan was unconcerned about his horns. Everyone had pointed ears, hairy feet, medieval dress, bad wigs, and light-sabers. Laura shivered. "What is this? Another dimension?"

Pan lowered his head and laughed. "This is a science fiction convention. They're fun for us, because we can be 'in costume.' Venus likes to attend these events . . . posing as herself."

He strode into the hotel lobby and grabbed a rather large woman clad in furs and chain mail. "Hello there, beautiful!" growled the satyr.

"Oh, honey, I remember those horns!" She laughed, running her fingers through his mane of silvery hair. "What are you supposed to be?"

"A randy goatman," answered Laura, stepping up beside them.

The chubby girl in lion skins giggled. "And you know, he looks just like one! He should enter the masquerade."

Laura looked pointedly at Pan. "Listen, before you ditch me, where do I find her?"

"She'll be dressed like a Greek goddess,"

the satyr answered. "Don't worry, when it comes to being noticed, Venus makes Narcissus look like Medusa."

"I want to see the art exhibit!" said another satyr, galloping in on his hooves. In a few moments, the satyr motorcycle gang was absorbed into the costumed swarm of fantasy and science fiction fans.

With a sigh, Laura adjusted her glasses and looked down at the skintight black leather outfit she was wearing. She didn't look like she was from Middle-earth, but she was dressed more bizarrely than usual. Maybe she would fit in after all.

"Have you seen Venus?" she asked every fan she bumped into.

"Not yet," came the answer. "Try the gamers' room."

She checked there and found no Venus, so she asked again, "Have you seen Venus?"

"Try the video room." Laura went up to the ballroom level and searched all the meeting rooms. For the next two hours, she searched every public corner of the hotel, and they finally made her buy a membership to the convention and wear a badge. A few people asked her what was in her duffel bag, and she claimed it was just her luggage.

Although they were dressed oddly, the people at the science fiction convention were extremely friendly. Most of them seemed to know Venus, and they said she came to this con every year. But she wasn't exactly punctual.

Laura roamed through the dealer's room, looking at the collectible toys, fantasy jewelry, movie posters, and old books. A friendly security guard came up and told her that she couldn't carry her bag into this room. Instead of checking it, she just took out the bow and quiver of arrows and wore them on her back. Laura didn't look much different than scores of fans who were wearing fanciful weapons.

She saw many mythical and marvelous characters, including the satyrs, who winked slyly at her, but no flamboyant goddess. At nine o'clock, she sat down in the hotel lobby to wait, figuring that Venus had to come this way to check in.

At this very moment, she mused, *the Homecoming football game is going on at Fimbrey High.* Laura was sad that it was her senior year, her last Homecoming, and she couldn't be there. The way things were going, she wasn't going to make the dance either.

Mercury sat in the living room of Cupidity's recently cleaned apartment, listening to the drone of the football game on the radio. Except for that noise, it was too quiet down the hallway near Cupidity's bedroom. He got up to investigate when he heard the door open, and he caught sight of a blond figure in a bathrobe dashing down the hall into the bathroom. All right, Cupidity was accounted for.

He hadn't seen his so-called daughter much since he had put her on restriction. Had she really been his daughter, Mercury might have felt bad about that, but he couldn't feel bad about punishing a deranged cherub.

Something seemed to happen in the football game, because he heard a shriek of delight. The messenger god sat back in his chair, thinking that Cupidity didn't understand football. She didn't know a halfback from a hunchback, so what was she cheering about?

Mercury rose to his feet again and

hobbled down the hall. As soon as he did, Cupidity again bolted out of her bedroom and into the bathroom. He didn't get a good look at her, because she moved like a track star.

He stopped at the bathroom door and asked, "Darling, are you all right?"

"Don't come in," she said in a muffled voice, covered by a sneeze. He didn't go in, but he marched down to her bedroom and went in there. The first thing Mercury did was look in her closet, where she had kept the gown she intended to wear to the dance. It was gone!

The anxious god heard the crackling sound of static, and he found a small black-and-white TV set hidden under her pillow. It was a security monitor, and the image showed the chair in which he had been sitting. They had been spying on him with a hidden camera! The window was also open several inches.

Those lousy teenagers, he thought, *they're worse than Harpies!*

Mercury didn't know who was in his bathroom, but he doubted whether it was Cupidity. This time he banged loudly on the bathroom door and shouted. "How long has she been gone?"

"Achooo!" came the response. "I can't hear you—the hair dryer is going!"

"You've been caught! I know Cupidity is gone. Now open up!"

Slowly the door creaked open, and a sheepish blond-haired girl stuck her head out. "Oh, please," she begged, "the dance meant so much to her. Let her go!"

"She's already there, isn't she?" muttered Mercury. "What's your name?"

"Chelsea," answered the chastened teen. "I just wanted to do her a favor . . . help her out. Everybody loves Cupidity—she's like the spirit of the school!"

"Yeah," grumbled the elder, "she's always been the life of the party. Did she go out the window, and was a car waiting for her?"

Chelsea nodded. "Cody brought me here, and we switched places. Don't be mad—they're like really in love!"

"I know." Mercury glanced at his watch and saw that it was ten o'clock. He scowled and started for the door. "Come on, I'll have my driver take us to the dance."

"It's going to be a madhouse at school," warned Chelsea, tossing away the robe to reveal that she was fully dressed. "The game is almost over."

"That's for sure," said Mercury with a sigh.

Laura was actually dozing in a big over-stuffed chair in the corner of the hotel lobby when a fresh babble of voices woke her up. She bolted upright, angry at herself for sleeping on the job, when she saw a mass of people swarm though the front door. At the center of this maelstrom was a tall, elegant woman in a cream-colored, diaphanous gown that swept behind her like a superhero's cape.

Members of her entourage descended on the check-in desk and the con desk, and it was obvious that a personage had arrived.

"Hello, Yoda! Hello, Captain Picard!" the raven-haired beauty called out to people. Even though the lobby was already crowded with fans, it got twice as crammed as people pressed forward to greet the new arrival. Many of them called her by name: "Venus."

Laura took a deep breath and rose from

the comfy chair. She moved the magical bow from her back to her front to make it easier to see, then she marched into the crush of people. As she got closer to her quarry, she could tell that Venus was of uncertain age, one of those well-preserved women somewhere between forty and four thousand years old.

"Venus!" she called.

"And who are you supposed to be?" asked the goddess snidely. "Lara Croft?"

People swarmed around them, but Laura pressed forward. "I'm trying to be Cupid."

"You don't look anything like Cupid," replied Venus with a scowl. She waved over Laura's head. "Gandalf, good to see you!"

"What about this bow?" asked Laura, holding up the weapon. "It's Cupid's bow!"

At first Venus rolled her eyes, then she narrowed them and took a closer look at the willowy weapon. "That's a good copy, but you still have a lousy costume."

Someone handed the dark-haired woman a convention badge that read, VENUS, and she carefully pinned it to her gown. "Who's got my room key?" she demanded.

"Right here!" said a member of her entourage, handing her a small envelope. When Venus and her crew began to make their way out of the lobby, Laura doggedly followed her.

"Venus!" she called. "Pan and his gang brought me here on their motorcycles . . . all the way from Pinkie's!"

Despite being caught up in the flow of people through the lobby, Venus stopped dead in her tracks. The goddess of love turned and cast a suspicious gaze at Laura. "You're beginning to annoy me."

"I just want five minutes of your time," promised the girl. "To tell you about what happened to Cupid."

Venus sniffed in disdain. "You obviously have me confused with someone who cares. I'm here to have fun. Be fun, or be gone!" The goddess gave her a dismissive wave and walked on.

The rejection plunged Laura into despair, and she again felt like a stalker as she followed Venus from one part of the convention to another. She could always use Cupid's bow to get her attention, but she couldn't risk getting into trouble with the law or security. Every room seemed to have a giant clock in it, and time was ticking off. It was almost ten thirty.

As the evening wore on, Venus and most of the revelers found their way to the hotel ballroom, where a Regency Dance was in progress. Laura watched glumly as people costumed in velvet finery from the court of England two centuries ago dipped and curtsied to baroque music from a string quartet. To Laura, it looked like elegant square dancing, with much touching of fingertips.

Laughing gaily, Venus joined the lines of courtly dancers, and she knew the archaic steps better than any of them. Watching them and thinking about the Homecoming Dance only depressed Laura. Time was running out, and she had to talk to the love goddess. She noticed that the participants were thrown together for a few seconds here and there, when they could converse.

So Laura took the plunge and jumped into the stately dance. She smiled a lot and tried to master the steps while she waited to come in contact with Venus.

More people from the audience joined in, and all of them were in the wrong costumes, too.

She was finally paired with Venus in the fingertip touching. "Oh, you again," said the goddess with a sneer. They curtsied and stepped back and forth in time to the music.

Laura laughed. "I've got a funny joke— I promise! There was this old cherub who smoked cigars, and Vulcan turned him into a hot teenage girl to go back to high school. Have you heard this one?"

"No," said Venus doubtfully, her stunning blue eyes peering at Laura.

In a rush, Laura blurted out the rest. "Cupidity is the hottest thing in high school, but her stupid friend shoots her with her own bow and arrow. How silly! Now Cupidity is in love with a skater boy and doesn't know who she really is."

Venus threw back her head and roared with laughter. "That *is* funny!"

The teen grabbed her hand and dragged her out of the line of dancers. "It gets even better," promised Laura. "At midnight tonight, Cupidity will turn back into this cherub, but who knows if she'll get her memory back."

"Who cares?" snapped Venus, pulling her arm away from the leather-clad biker chick. "It's every god for himself."

"Oh, please," begged Laura, giving up any pretense, "help me! Cupidity will be right in the middle of getting crowned Homecoming Queen, and a good friend of mine is in love with the wrong girl. And—and—" Breathlessly she tried to collect her thoughts before the goddess fled from the ballroom.

Venus frowned and said, "Wait a minute; they're crowning a queen of this dance, and it's going to be Cupid?"

Laura's eyes widened, and she realized the chink in Venus's armor. "You mean Cupidity," said the mortal, "that's who she is now. She's the most gorgeous female on the planet, and she's also madly in love—from her own stupid arrows. So she's got that glow thing working. At our Homecoming Dance, we always crown the most beautiful woman in the world as queen. That could only be Cupidity."

"More gorgeous than *me?*" asked Venus with astonishment.

Laura pondered the question. "That would be hard to say, unless I saw the two of you standing together." Laura looked up at the clock over the door. "We could still make it to the festival by midnight. It's only ten forty-five now, and it's right next door in Ohio."

"Ohio?" asked the goddess thoughtfully. "Yes, but Indiana is in the Central Time Zone, and Ohio is in the Eastern Time Zone. It's an hour later in Ohio—it's a quarter 'til midnight."

"Oh no!" sputtered Laura, grabbing her wrist. "We've got to rush, we've got to go!"

"Let me call my brother," said Venus, reaching under her gown and pulling out a cell phone.

Fourteen

After fighting horrendous traffic, crazed football fans, and a person selling tickets who didn't want to let him in, Mercury finally entered the high school gymnasium. It was just as chaotic inside as out, and he could hardly believe this Homecoming event had been organized by adults. On stage, a rock band blasted music that made his teeth hurt, but the laughter and conversation threatened to drown out the band. Strobe lights, fog machines, and balloons didn't do anything to help his vision or his mood.

There were hordes of kids, mostly standing around in large packs and doing precious little dancing. It was so dark that he wondered why any of them had bothered with the fancy outfits they were wearing. The gangly boys looked ridiculous in suits and tuxedos, although some of the young ladies looked fetching in their gowns. None of the girls were quite as delectable as Cupidity, but he couldn't find the cherub anywhere.

Of course Chelsea had deserted him as soon as they entered the place, and she had probably run off to warn Cupidity that he was there. *Patience,* he told himself, *I'll find her.* After all, the gymnasium was massive, and the students washed back and forth across the floor like the tide.

Mercury was dressed well enough to fit in with this exuberant crowd, as long as he kept to the shadows. He stalked the refreshment tables, looking for Cupidity but not finding her. He returned to the entrance, where the couples were having their pictures taken under a harvest archway of squashes, corn, and pinecones.

The elder asked nicely for Cupidity but was told that she and Cody had gotten their pictures taken earlier. Every couple was automatically entered for King and Queen, but the votes were already counted by now. As Laura Sweeney had told him, there were a great many mismatched couples at the dance, possibly more victims of Cupid's troublesome arrows.

The god of punctuality checked his watch and saw that it was ten minutes until midnight. With any luck, Cupidity would be hiding from him when the hour struck, and everyone would be spared having to witness her transformation. How would they ever explain that away? He could affect mortals' minds but only on a small scale, not a gymnasium crammed with hundreds of people.

Wincing from the noise, he looked around, realizing that Laura was not going to return with Venus in time to help matters. Well, that had been a long shot, anyway. Such a mess as this was bound to end in disaster. With any luck, maybe it would only be a small-scale disaster.

The gruesome song ended with a discordant chord that made Mercury grit his teeth. In the silence that followed, he tried to collect his thoughts, but a loud drumroll shattered the brief calm.

"Fimbrey rocks!" shouted the lead singer to raucous applause. "Students of Fimbrey High, it's almost midnight—are you having a good time?"

"Yeah!" they bellowed back.

"To announce the Homecoming King and Queen, here is your principal, Denise Waterbury!" The singer stepped back to allow a middle-aged woman to take the microphone, and the crowd began to press closer to get a better look. Spotlights bathed the stage, showing that the principal was dressed in a proper business suit, bringing a touch of class to the chaotic proceedings.

The principal beamed with pride. "Students of Fimbrey High," she began, "this year's attendance at the Homecoming Dance is almost double last year's attendance. It's wonderful! I've seen so many faces I've never seen before at any of our events, although I do see you in my office from time to time."

There was polite laughter, and the principal went on, "I am truly pleased by the diversity I've seen tonight. In fact, the last few weeks. I know we've had a few strange incidents around school, but overall problems have been down. And our football team scored a touchdown tonight and only lost by ten points. Let's give them a big hand!"

When that got scattered boos, Mrs. Waterbury plunged on. "So let me announce our Homecoming King and Queen. We counted all the votes, but we hardly needed to. It was a landslide! You know them as a perfectly darling couple, and it's hard to believe that one of them came to our school just a few weeks ago. I can't imagine Fimbrey without her. Our Homecoming Queen—Cupidity Larraine!"

The audience applauded wildly as the stunning, fair-haired beauty sauntered toward the microphone. The lights caught her sparkling skintight gown and her shimmering skin and hair. She looked unreal—an apparition concocted by gods. Mercury could understand how all of these people had been fooled, all of them except Laura Sweeney.

"And the Homecoming King," announced the principal, "Cody Kenyon!"

Dressed in an Edwardian tux and looking impossibly rakish, the skateboarder strode onto the stage to wild applause. Mercury had to admit, his brooding dark looks contrasted nicely with Cupidity's sunny appeal. Who could deny that they were the King and Queen of this rowdy lot of mortals?

A gaggle of girls and a mob of boys rushed forward to clamp crowns on their heads, and Cupidity giggled into the microphone. The petite blond had to stand on tiptoes to reach the device, and every male in the audience stood on tiptoes to watch her.

"This is such an honor!" she yelled to much cheering and stomping. "You could have picked Megan and Peter, or Emma and Jake . . . or so many others. Kisses!" She promptly took time out in her speech to blow kisses at her beaming friends.

Mercury's watch buzzed, and he groaned as he turned off the alarm. *Already midnight,* he thought ruefully.

Cupidity sniffed back a big tear, and it sounded like a goose honking. "I never thought I would be welcomed so warmly in my new school," she declared in a hoarse voice. "It makes me forget about all the other places I've ever lived . . . wherever they were! Here I've found true love and friendship. I see you, Papa!"

She waved directly at Mercury, and he tried not to cringe. "Kiss her!" shouted the crowd. "Kiss her, Cody!"

This was apparently a rite that everybody eagerly awaited, and Cody wasn't going to disappoint. He scooped Cupidity up in his arms, and all of her hair promptly fell out, showering the first row in silvery strands that glinted in the spotlight. Some in the crowd shrieked, but Cody was oblivious. He pressed home with his kiss, even as her body writhed and twisted in his arms.

Cupidity's silky skin turned cracked and hairy, and bits of her perfect body crumbled off. Trying to kiss her, Cody looked as if he were wrestling an alligator, and the audience screamed in alarm. They shook one another in disbelief, and a boy near Mercury fainted and fell to the floor.

Finally Cody heard the screaming and realized something was wrong. When he drew back, he saw a shriveled, wizened cherub in a lumpy evening dress that was tight only across the belly. Cody screamed louder than any of the girls, and Mercury couldn't blame him. Grizzled, bald-headed Cupid looked like a lawn statue that had been left out in the rain too long.

"What's the matter?" asked Cupid in a gruff voice. "What's the matter, Codykins?"

The skater was clawing his way off the stage, as were most of his friends, when Mercury felt a tug on his sleeve. "Hi, Dad," said a familiar voice.

The god turned to see his oldest son. "Pan!" he exclaimed happily. "What are you doing here?"

"I had to drive the chariot," answered the satyr, "to get the ladies here. That mortal did it—she talked Venus into coming—but I guess we're too late."

"Where are they?" asked Mercury, peering over the heads of the panicked crowd.

"Near the stage!" The satyr pointed into the turmoil.

Laura froze on the steps leading up to the stage, and she didn't know whether to cry, laugh, or scream like everybody else was doing. They were going to be traumatized for years after seeing the hottest girl in the school morph into a gnarly little gnome. Laura had been expecting it, but even she could hardly stand to look at the creature that was left after Cupidity dissolved. This was like a Japanese horror movie, when the pretty moth turns into an ugly monster everyone wants to destroy.

When she tore her eyes away from the stage, Laura saw the horrified faces of Peter, Megan, Emma, and Jake. She wanted to run to Peter's side and comfort him, but they all probably figured they were losing their minds.

"Where's Cupidity?" wailed Cody, dropping to his knees and shaking his fists at the cherub. *"What have you done to her?"*

"Get a grip, dude!" ordered Cupid, scowling. "Everyone, settle down. I'm not done with my speech!"

"He still has no memory," said a voice behind Laura. She turned to look at the impossibly beautiful Venus, who now would have no problem being elected queen of this terrified mob. "Damn, I'm going to have to step in here, aren't I?"

Laura looked pleadingly at her. "If you do a good deed, I promise never to tell anyone."

Venus gave a hollow laugh. "You'd better not—that would ruin my reputation. First we have to break the love spells. Hand me an arrow."

"You have to be careful with them," warned Laura, feeling possessive about her magical weapon.

"Don't argue with me, mortal!" snapped Venus. "Who's the goddess here? I've done this before, okay? So hand me an arrow."

This time Laura quickly obeyed, fishing an arrow out of Cupid's quiver and handing it to the raven-haired goddess of love. With pandemonium, screaming, and shouting all around them, Venus held Cupid's arrow between her two clenched fists and chanted in an ancient tongue.

Maybe it was the fog machine or the strobe lights, but the room began to spin. Strange flashes sparkled in the air, and Laura felt dizzy. She eased herself onto the steps as other students knelt in dazed confusion. Through blurry vision, she looked for Cupid and saw the grizzled cherub stagger and fall down. He was also under Venus's spell.

With a loud yelp, the goddess snapped the arrow in two, and the shaft disappeared in her hands. Laura still felt dazed, but the spinning went away. She staggered to her feet and looked at the goddess of love, who was breathing heavily.

"Mama!" yelled a raspy voice. "Mama!"

"Yes, my baby!" Venus leaped to her feet and ran up the stairs to embrace her frightened son, even though he was a shriveled cherub wearing a sparkly evening gown. "It's all right, baby, I'll take you home!"

The cherub pointed accusingly at Laura. "Mama, she's got my bow and arrows! She *took* them without asking!"

"No, you let Laura play with them," said Venus. "That's your friend, remember? But she will have to give them back now."

"Is that it?" asked Laura, taking the bow and quiver of arrows off her leather-clad shoulder. She felt oddly naked without them. "Everything is back to normal?"

Venus gave Cupid back his bow. "What's

your definition of normal?" she asked. "I don't know how much they'll remember, but Cupid's spell is broken. Anyone in love now is honestly in love."

With those words ringing in her ears, Laura searched the area for Peter Yarmench. She spotted him backstage, arguing with Jake, and the two boys were almost back to blows as they had been on that afternoon so long ago.

"I caught you looking at her!" accused Jake. "You stay away from my girlfriend!"

Peter looked in confusion from Megan to Emma, and the girls gazed back at him. "Which one is your girlfriend?" asked Peter.

"Why, it's—" Jake paused, pointing first at the head cheerleader, then at the pale goth chick dressed in a spider-web black dress.

"It's me, dummy!" declared Megan, putting her hands on her hips. "I was only with Peter to . . . to make you jealous."

Emma just shook her head in confusion and looked as if she wanted to hide. "I don't know, Jake. I thought we had some-thing . . . but it's up to you."

"Tell this ghoul to get lost!" insisted

Megan, staring daggers at Emma.

Jake seemed to come to an epiphany, and he shook his head. "I don't think so. I need to look outside the box, like Cupidity told me. I'm with Emma." He rushed to the goth's side and put his arm around her waist. "See ya, Megan."

"Ack! Ack!" The queen bee could barely talk, and she started hyperventilating in shock.

Laura gazed in amazement at Jake and Emma as they hugged each other happily. Cupid's arrows made no difference to them—they were really in love. In fact, most of the mismatched romances at the Homecoming Dance seemed to be genuine.

Laura found herself gravitating to Peter's side. Did he really like her, or was he still lovesick and confused? He had just lost his date for the evening, and she knew how that felt.

"Peter, are you okay?" she asked with concern.

He looked appreciatively at her skin-tight leather ensemble. "Wow, that is some hot outfit! Do you always go to dances dressed like a biker babe?"

She smiled. "I didn't have a date, so I crashed this place with my motorcycle gang."

Peter looked around and whispered, "Would you hate me forever if I ditched my date and hung out with you?"

"No," she said with a grin, "but this is the last time you get to do that."

"Where's Cupidity?" yelled a forlorn voice. "Where did she go?" They all turned to see Cody Kenyon shuffling through the crowd of people, a dazed look on his face and a lopsided crown on his head.

"Dude," said Jake, "she bailed on you after you kissed some ugly little guy."

"Yeah," replied Emma. "I don't blame her."

In sympathy, Megan grabbed Cody's arm and escorted him away from the others. "Come on, Cody, let's ditch these losers. I'll take care of you."

"More music!" yelled the principal, trying to get the dance back on track. "Rockers, can't we have some more tunes?"

"Yes, Mrs. Waterbury," responded the lead singer, trying to gather up his band. "Come on, people, everyone off the stage but the musicians!"

Peter grabbed Laura's hand and led her down the stairs and across the dance floor, where they ran into Taryn and Chester. "Laura!" shouted Taryn with a delirious squeal. "I *knew* you'd make it to the dance, and you're here with Peter. See, I told you everything would work out!"

"Are you guys okay?" asked Laura with concern.

"Never better," answered Chester, gripping Taryn by the waist. "Laura, you have to wear kinky leather more often—you look hot." He gave Peter a playful thumbs-up sign.

Suddenly the band started playing again, and it was impossible to talk over the din. Hand in hand, Peter and Laura wound their way through the throng of people until they were outside, and the brisk night air felt like a welcome dash of cold water in Laura's face.

"Make a wish," said Peter, touching her arm. "There's a shooting star—a big one."

She looked up to see an impressive light flash across the night sky, although she knew it was too big and too bright to be a meteorite. "Apollo's chariot," she answered with a wave. "Good-bye, friends."

"I'm not going anywhere," said Peter, putting his arm around her. "I'm happy right here."

"Me, too," agreed Laura, nuzzling his shoulder.

As Peter leaned down and gently brushed his lips against hers, Laura felt a shiver leap through her body. As they kissed for the first time under the glimmering sky, she realized that love didn't just come from a bow and arrow. Sometimes, it was written in the stars.

LOL at this sneak peek of
South Beach Sizzle
By Suzanne Weyn and Diana Gonzalez

A New Romantic Comedy from Simon Pulse

"Okay, so what if your first day at work will someday be made into a disaster movie starring Ashton Kutcher and Hilary Duff?" Jeff said later that day. It was about six o'clock and they were walking along Ocean Drive on the beach side. "At least she didn't fire you."

"I think she was afraid to come too close to me," Lula replied. "She was probably afraid to be sucked into the black hole of disaster that I had become. It didn't stop all day. I spilled things. I got orders mixed up. I even forgot to give someone the check and they left without paying."

Jeff chuckled. "At least you *have* a job. I got laughed out of some of the best restaurants in Sobe today."

"Sobe?" she asked.

"Yes, That what those of us who are in the know call South Beach," he explained. "And now *you* know what those in the know know, ya know?"

"I guess I know," she agreed, laughing.

They stopped in front of a clothing store. "This place sells bathing suits," he pointed out.

Despite all her mishaps, Lula had earned thirty dollars in tips at lunch. She had no bathing suit and so she and Jeff were now on a mission to find one. "Remember," he said as he pulled open the door to the store. "Don't pick out something that says 'Mother Theresa at the Seashore' all over it."

"I'm not the type of girl who has to show everything I've got," she insisted.

"No kidding," he agreed. "I'm still in shock from your last bathing suit."

"You mean that cute suit with the knee-length board shorts and short-sleeved top?"

"That's the one," he replied. "The only thing missing was the little ruffled swim bonnet."

"I would have packed that suit but I

could never find it again after that day I wore it to Coney Island with you."

"I have a confession," he said. "You couldn't find it because I threw it in the incinerator. I saw it on a chair in your apartment one day and just thought, 'What the heck. She'll thank me some day.' After all, what are gay guy friends for, if not to save you from your worst fashion mistakes?"

"You burned my bathing suit?" Lula cried, aghast.

"Yes. Not to worry, that's why I'm generously offering to help you pick out a new one—a much better one," he said, guiding her into the store. "Someday when I'm *filthy rich* again, I'll even offer to pay for it."

Inside, Lula looked through a rack of Speedo tank suits, while Jeff brought over bikinis he thought would look good on her. After she refused the tenth bikini offering, he gave up. "You're hopeless," he told her. "I'm going to go look in the men's department."

"Happy hunting," she said as he wandered off. She pushed a few more suits down the rack and picked one out, but she couldn't keep her mind on shopping. Maybe Jeff was right. It was possible that her style needed a little shaking up. She realized she was holding a black tank suit in her hand.

She put it back and went over to the two-piece rack. Pushing aside a group of hot pink and lime green string bikinis, she looked for something with a little more coverage.

After trying on four suits, she settled on a denim fabric two-piece with a halter top and board shorts. "Perfect," said Jeff appearing from behind a rack. "I'm proud of you for showing your *girlage* a little."

He came alongside her and leaned in close. "Don't be obvious," he said in a low tone. "But shift your drift to the right by the flip-flops over there."

Lula pretended to stretch and casually glanced to the right. She froze mid stretch.

Standing in front of the flip-flop rack was the hottest hottie she'd ever laid eyes on. He was about six foot, maybe a little taller. Broad shoulders muscled out from under a black T-shirt. His jeans weren't too tight, but tight enough to give a truly inspiring view.

"Whoa," she breathed out, letting her arms drop.

He turned their way as though sensing the attention they'd focused on him. Large dark eyes took them in and his white teeth glinted slightly when he smiled.

Jeff and Lula both smiled back, dazed and confused by the brilliance of his looks. *We must look like two escapees from the psycho ward,* Lula realized.

Despite that, she couldn't stop staring at him as he walked away from the flip-flops to the front counter. "Did you see how he was totally checking me out?" Jeff whispered.

"Dream on," Lula disagreed. "He was smiling at me."

Lula watched him head toward the front door and—just before he walked out—he stopped and looked over at them.

He was interested in . . . one of them. *Let it be me, let it be me,* she found herself feverishly hoping as she went back to the rack and reconsidered the hot pink string bikini.

Sign up for the CHECK YOUR PULSE
free teen e-mail book club!

 **FEATURING**

A new book discussion every month

Monthly book giveaways

Chapter excerpts

Book discussions with the authors

Literary horoscopes

Plus YOUR comments!

To sign up go to www.simonsays.com/simonpulse and
don't forget to CHECK YOUR PULSE!